THE LAST ALBION

ANDREW RAYMOND

Copyright © 2024 by Andrew Raymond

All rights reserved.

No part of this book may be reproduced in any form or by any electronic or mechanical means, including information storage and retrieval systems, without written permission from the author, except for the use of brief quotations in a book review.

All characters in this publication are fictitious and any resemblance to real persons, living or dead, is purely coincidental.

ALSO BY ANDREW RAYMOND

Novak and Mitchell

1. Official Secrets

2. Capitol Spy

3. Traitor Games

4. True Republic

5. Blood Money (final book in the series)

DCI John Lomond – a Scottish crime series

1. The Bonnie Dead

2. The Shortlist

3. The Bloody, Bloody Banks

4. Cold Open

Duncan Grant

1. Kill Day

2. Dead Flags

3. The Last Albion

Standalone

The Limits of the World

CHAPTER ONE

CARBIS BAY, CORNWALL – SUNDAY MORNING

On a chilly but sunny morning in her clifftop garden, overlooking Carbis Bay in Cornwall, seventy-six-year-old Sheila Hayworth rooted through her wax canvas gardening bag. Then she shuffled her Glock 19 Gen5 pistol aside to find her trowel.

Like any other day, she wasn't expecting trouble. Carbis Bay didn't see much in the way of trouble, other than some sunburned tourists on the beach far below. But old habits die hard.

Sheila kneeled on her foam mat alongside her bed of daylilies and geraniums. As she tended the soil and inspected the flowers, she zoned out, staring at the red and orange colours. She was now seeing blood pouring out of a man's back, turning the snow in an alleyway crimson. There were places like that alleyway that Sheila would never forget. If taken back to Moscow even all those decades later, she could still have found it on memory alone.

That was the great thing about retirement. If Sheila wished, she never had to go back to any of those places that haunted her memories and her dreams. She had long since made peace with the fact that she would always have them. It was the trade-off with the life she had chosen.

Behind her, a voice called out from the wooden fence that ran around the side of her house. 'Excuse me, sorry to bother you...'

Sheila snapped out of her daze and turned around. The voice was benign and pleasant, so she didn't have any immediate cause for concern. Then she realised: how did they get past the locked gate before the fence?

'Can I help you?' Sheila asked, getting to her feet.

The man was tall, but could still barely see over the fence.

All Sheila could really make out was a pair of eyes and a balding head. The man was in his sixties. 'Yeah,' he said, 'I was looking for Angela Spencer.'

Sheila froze. It had been a long time since anyone had ever called her that. She let out a sad exhalation, realising what was about to happen. 'I don't suppose it would do me any good to cry for help.'

Sheila recoiled as she saw a dark figure in her peripheral vision burst out of the bushes that marked the perimeter of her garden. He was hooded and had his arm extended, holding a pistol with a suppressor attached to the end.

Before Sheila could do anything else, the man fired two shots into the side of her head.

The impact of the shots sent her head rocketing sideways, swiftly followed by the rest of her body.

The hooded man ran over to her crumpled body, then fired more rounds into her head and torso, then he disappeared back into the bushes.

The man by the fence was already gone.

Hillhead, Glasgow – Monday morning

It was a drizzly morning in the upmarket West End of Glasgow. Mothers pottered around with yoga mats under their arms, sipping from takeaway coffee cups. Courier vans and bikers took up most of the parking spaces on Byres Road as the week sluggishly got into gear.

At eleven o'clock, fifty-two-year-old James Docherty was only just unlocking the front door of Docherty Books. Like every other day, he stumbled in the front door, tripping on the large pile of books that had fallen over in the middle of the night. He had been aware of the pile for months, and claimed to himself he would do something about them. Only now that the pile was actually impeding anyone coming or going did he finally tidy them away.

The morning was like any other. He sat behind a large wooden desk at the far end of the shop, giving him a clear view of anyone entering. Not that he ever greeted a customer. Everyone was met with a similar level of disdain or suspicion. In fact, customers were treated by Docherty as an annoyance who interrupted whatever old spy novel he was engrossed in.

The shop was musty, smelled of cat food, and there were unruly stacks of books everywhere. None of them alphabetised. Spines turned the wrong way around, and the books kept in only the vaguest of subject groupings.

Settled in for the day with a coffee flask filled with whisky, and a tattered copy of James Buchan's *The Thirty-Nine Steps* in his hands, Docherty tutted to himself as he heard the bell of the front door ring. A male Chinese student entered.

He had his bag double-strapped over his shoulders, and a

keen, motivated look about him. Specificity was the worst trait to enter Docherty Books with. Docherty himself had little knowledge of what exactly was in his store or where. And Docherty just knew the student was going to ask him for something specific. A downside of being so close to Glasgow University. The international students who didn't know any better mistook the place for an actual, proper bookshop, with computerised inventory, organised shelving, and friendly customer service.

'Excuse me,' the student began earnestly, still halfway down the shop. 'I'm looking for...'

Docherty squinted. He couldn't make out the request. Thinking he'd been asked for Walter Scott, he shook his head and pointed to an unsorted pile on the floor near the student. 'I saw some Walter Scott around there a few months ago. Have a rummage through it.'

The student looked at the pile in confusion, then back again at Docherty. 'No, sorry, not Walter Scott...'

Docherty might have been drunk by lunchtime, but there were still some elements of his old skills that he had access to. Instincts. This wasn't any other Chinese student. There was a grittiness to his expression. The innocence in his voice replaced with something far more driven. Confident. And real.

The student clarified, 'I'm looking for William Stott.'

It was a name that very few people in the world knew. The fact that it was being uttered to Docherty couldn't have been a coincidence.

Docherty nodded solemnly. 'Before you do it, can you tell me...is it because of Vienna? Or Madrid?'

The student took out a pistol with a suppressor attached. 'Don't know. Don't care.' Then he fired a shot into Docherty's forehead.

The force of the bullet sent Docherty straight backwards, his light wooden chair upended. The student hurried quickly over and fired three more shots into him.

On his way out, he turned the Open sign on the front door around to show the shop as Closed. Then he seamlessly joined the other student traffic on Byres Road.

Victoria Park, Newbury – Wednesday morning

It was a busy park in the morning, with mothers, fathers, grandparents, and carers descending on the play park with buggies and toddlers. The cries of laughter and fun rang out all around, across the nearby canal and bandstand.

Further away from the crowds at the north end, a safe distance from the many dog walkers, was a man in unseasonable shorts and t-shirt. He was lifting and lowering a kettlebell above his head, demonstrating the correct form.

Facing him was an overweight man, huffing and puffing with each rep. Despite the chill in the air, he was pouring sweat.

The trainer, Jez, by contrast, looked fresh as a daisy. It was a workout he could have done twice as fast, several times through the day – and he did. As a freelance trainer, the park was his office. It was an ideal place, free from rent, and if the weather ever turned, he made it part of the appeal – that by training with him in the outdoors, the clients convinced themselves they were putting in a bit more effort than someone who showed up in the evenings to an air-conditioned corporate gym filled with expensive machines and thumping chart music. Roughing it in the park was part of Jez's unique selling point.

'Come on,' Jez encouraged, 'one more rep, Ollie...'

Ollie tensed his core, trying to lift the kettlebell one more time. But try as he might, through a guttural groan, he couldn't lift his arm any higher. He relented, releasing the kettlebell, which landed on the soft, damp grass with a thud. 'I can't,' he puffed, leaning over his knees. His vision turned dark and cloudy.

Jez could see him struggling with his balance, and reached over to him. 'Hey, you okay?' He encouraged Ollie to stand up straight.

As his vision cleared, Ollie thought he might throw up. Instead, his attention turned to a man jogging nearby.

Seeing Ollie distracted, Jez looked around. It immediately felt wrong. In the vastness of the park, the man was jogging much closer than he needed to.

Anxious, and knowing in his gut that something was wrong, Jez patted Ollie on the back. 'Let's wrap it up there for the day.'

Exhausted but surprised, Ollie said, 'Already? It's only been twenty minutes.'

Keeping tabs on the jogger without making deliberate eye contact, Jez said, 'Yeah, I don't think you should push any harder today. Let's go get something to drink.'

Jez quickly packed up the kettlebells and loaded them onto the push trolley he used for carting equipment about. He led Ollie south, trying to get back amongst people as soon as possible. But the cart was getting stuck in the mud.

Jez kept looking over his shoulder, seeing the jogger coming in the same direction, but maintaining the same distance.

Just when Jez wanted to push on and get closer to the play park, Ollie stopped and leaned over his knees again.

'Hang on,' Ollie grumbled, taking off his backpack. 'Sorry, I think I'm going to throw up...'

While Jez checked where the jogger was once more, he didn't notice Ollie pulling a knife out of his backpack. By the time he realised what was happening, Ollie had already slit Jez's throat.

He ran off towards the jogger, heading for the exit at the north end of the park.

Jez was left stricken in the middle of a huge expanse of grass, sprawled and spluttering over his cart. The blood was everywhere. He knew he was bleeding out.

What he didn't understand was why. He had been out of the game for five years.

Why did someone want him dead now?

CHAPTER TWO

Blackness surrounded Duncan Grant. Everywhere he looked, it enveloped him. Even as he drove at over seventy miles an hour along the Isle of Skye's A851 and then the A87 with his headlights off late at night.

The A roads were the closest thing to a motorway on the island, unlit apart from the smattering of isolated settlements and villages that provided only pockets of light amid the jagged mountain ranges of the Cuillins, the vast expanse of peat bogs and conifer forests around Drumfearn, and the swathes of farmland to the north in the Trotternish peninsula. The place Grant had always called home.

Relying on his ingrained memories of the roads, he charged through the night without a thought or care for his safety. He knew every bend, every rise and fall, and every sudden hairpin. Still, he knew he was putting his life on the line driving at such insane speeds on twisting roads. He passed traffic like it was standing still, closing in on their red rear lights, and overtaking before the driver even realised Grant had been there. All they saw was a faint outline of a battered silver Vauxhall Belmont, along with a rush of wind as Grant raced past. Then he was gone into the night again.

It wasn't that Grant had a death wish. It had started by accident. Leaving his cottage in Trotternish and driving for five minutes before realising his headlights hadn't been on. There was something freeing about it. Of no longer having to worry about the risks. Gradually, he stepped harder and harder on the accelerator. The harder he pressed and the faster his speed climbed, the more alive Grant felt – despite the fact that he was inching himself closer and closer to death by doing so.

He just wanted to feel something – anything – other than what he had been feeling for the past month. So much had happened since his last operation, and yet also so little.

Having been evacuated from Saudi Arabia by Fifteen Flags operatives, Grant hadn't called in as MI6 had expected. It had left his handler, Leo Winston, in the dark about whether Grant had even survived. There didn't seem to be any point, as far as Grant saw it. Everything he had worked for, everything he had sacrificed in order to carve out a career in MI6 as an elite operative had been for nothing. It had become clear to Grant that he had been playing a rigged game from the start. He had joined MI6 to try and make a difference in the world. To do what he could to keep people safer. But for every operation that was a success, MI6 and the British government itself threatened to undermine every move Grant made.

After a few weeks, Grant was convinced that his time with MI6 had come to an end. He would instead live a life of quiet dedication on a farm, tending to crops and animals rather than the whims of politicians and intelligence agency bureaucrats. But as time marched on, there was a feeling that he couldn't shake.

The pain in his heart of losing Gretchen – the only person

he could say he had ever truly loved – reached a crescendo as he thought of her final expression as Henry Marlow shot her. It was a look of acceptance. Knowing that no matter what she could have done, it was always going to turn out that way: dying in some foreign land, by the hand of a man who had once been on the side of good. Just like Grant.

He accelerated further as he entered the tiny village of Uig. Light emanating from the small cottages that lined the right side of the road illuminated just enough of the roadside for Grant to see the sharp right-hand turn-off for Staffin. His tyres skidded as he slammed on the brakes. Grant threw the car around the corner, then floored the accelerator once more, climbing up the narrow road that snaked through the trees, up the steep single-track road. Climbing, climbing, until the cottages and crofts and the Uig pier were far below. Grant sent the car drifting into the switchback corner at the top of the hill, immediately being met with a wall of white light from an oncoming truck. There was nowhere for the truck to go, but Grant somehow managed to make an evasive manoeuvre in and then out of a ditch, scraping the left side of his car along a granite wall. The truck driver leaned on his horn out of pure anger.

The close call snapped Grant out of whatever broken state of mind he had been in for the last hour or two. Until then, the only person he had come close to putting in harm's way was himself. Now that others were coming increasingly into danger, Grant backed off on the speed. Once he came down to a mere forty miles an hour, he put on his headlights and slowed further.

He didn't want to hurt himself or anyone else. Gretchen wouldn't have wanted him to. Not on her account. Grant knew who needed to hurt. Who needed to pay. Not just for

Gretchen, but for Kadir Rashid – the innocent journalist who had dared to shed light on Foreign Secretary John Wark's dirty financial dealings with Saudi tyrant Crown Prince Mohammad bin Abdul. Rashid hadn't survived long enough to see his story in print. Then there was Henry Marlow, the man who would have died for his country and MI6 – only to become disillusioned by those who used his assassination skills to further their own personal ambitions rather than to safeguard the British people.

Grant wanted to make amends for them all.

Starting tonight.

CHAPTER THREE

When Grant got back to his cottage on the Trotternish coastline, he called a number that no one else in the world had. A private MI6 director's line.

Walking back through the streets of Westminster was MI6 Director of the Albion programme Leo Winston. When he saw the "*NUMBER WITHHELD*" caller ID, he stopped walking.

'Leo,' he answered, then waited a few charged seconds for a response.

Finally, Grant asked, 'Can you talk?'

'Where are you?' asked Winston.

Grant paused. 'Back home. Skye.'

'I've had people checking.'

'I know.'

'You need to come in, Duncan.'

'I'm not coming in.'

Winston sighed disconsolately. 'Grant, listen to me. You have to. Olivia told me today that there's going to be an enquiry.'

'About Marlow?'

Winston snapped. 'About Marlow, about the money – everything, Grant! Everything!' He closed his eyes and tried to take a calming breath. 'They're going to suspend me.'

'Of course they are,' said Grant. 'It's never the ones at fault who pay.'

'Randall got the money back. The slush fund cash that Marlow stole from Vauxhall Cross.'

'How did he manage that?'

Winston laughed darkly. 'He figured out the decryption code. Six figures. Guess what it was.'

'I couldn't begin to.'

'One two three four five six.'

Grant said nothing. It was Marlow's last laugh. One last laugh into the abyss.

Winston went on, 'The Foreign Sec doesn't care. He wants your head, Grant. The money was still in play when you shot Henry Marlow.'

'That was the job I was given,' replied Grant.

'Yeah, well...you and me both, mate.'

Grant said, 'I was in my car tonight, driving around the island. It was pitch black, and I realised after five minutes that I'd been driving without my lights on. I pressed the accelerator, speeding up and speeding up. I couldn't see a thing. The only thing keeping me on the road was my memory. I didn't care anymore. I just wanted...to feel something. Something other than this. That was when I realised what has to happen now. Who's to blame for all of this. For Kadir Rashid. Marlow. And now Gretchen. I'm going to find them. I won't stop until they're in the ground.'

Winston paused. 'Duncan, I know you must be very upset right now. Why don't I come up to see you?'

'By the time you get here I'll be gone.'

'Duncan–'

'Do you think I'm broken, Leo? Is that it? I am *not* broken. I've never seen things so clearly in my life. They're going to pay.'

Grant hung up.

At the other end, Winston held on, until eventually the line went dead. There was plenty on his mind. Not least that he had just broken four years of sobriety for only two sips of beer. That fact that he'd broken it at all now meant that all bets were off about what would happen to him. Whether he would even see the next morning was no longer a guarantee. Because that's what came with being an alcoholic. As long as Winston drank, absolutely anything could happen. Nothing was off the table. Not even suicide.

That was the terrible paradox for Leo Winston of being an alcoholic: without booze, he couldn't feel alive. But the only time he could ever contemplate suicide was when he drank. Thoughts of it crept up on him the more he drank. He had broken his sobriety now, after four of the most painful years of his life. The thought that harder years might still be ahead of him was enough for him to want to throw the towel in. There was no denying those two sips of beer. He couldn't pretend they had never happened. It wasn't about being able to lie to someone else about his sobriety. What mattered most was knowing in himself what he had done. And he *knew* that he had taken a drink.

All this and so much more rushed through his head, like a car speeding through a dark countryside road. He was a car with its lights off. Where he would end up now was anyone's guess. Because Winston knew from experience that because of those two tiny sips of beer, he had given himself permission to drink for the rest of the night. It didn't matter that the sensible thing to do was stop. To say, I know what happens from here and none of it is good. If I stop now, I can still save what remains of my life.

But that's not how it works for an alcoholic.

Winston stared at his phone, wishing Grant was still there. Then he said, 'I need help.'

With no one to hear his plea, Winston pocketed his phone. He set off again as if nothing was wrong. Then he veered off the pavement into the first available shop that sold booze. He sailed straight up to the counter, which was surrounded by walls of sweets – Winston only had eyes for the booze behind the counter.

He pointed to a bottle of Jack Daniels. 'That one, please,' he said, like someone picking out a stray in a cage from a dog home.

He made it another fifty yards from the shop before he peeled off the label on the bottle cap.

Now, all bets were off.

CHAPTER FOUR

WHAT WINSTON DIDN'T KNOW WAS that the moment the barmaid in the King's Arms had spotted the two sips missing from Winston's pint of beer, she called Barry the bar manager.

'Hi Barry, it's Alison,' she said, holding her other ear to block out the din of shouted conversation and music that dominated the background of the bar in typical Friday night fashion. 'I'm sorry to bother you on your night off, but you asked me to tell you if that guy came in.'

'Is he all right?' Barry asked with concern.

'He seems fine. He's just left, in fact. He barely touched his pint.'

Barely, thought Barry. He ended the call as quickly as he could, then scrolled through his contacts. He knew exactly what to do in the circumstances. The instructions had been made clear to him one quiet afternoon before he had even opened for the day. There was something about the woman that suggested he would be foolish not to follow her instructions to the letter.

He found the contact name under "LEO SPONSOR" then made the call.

Across the city in a Chelsea townhouse, Olivia Christie had only just removed her shoes in the hallway when she heard a phone ringing in her bedroom. It was a call she'd hoped to never get.

Christie found the burner phone in her bedside cabinet, placed there as she had always assumed that if Leo needed her help it would likely be in the dead of night. She answered and listened to Barry's description of what had happened.

He had no idea he was talking to the director of MI6, though he sometimes wondered who a man like Leo Winston would trust with the knowledge he was a recovering alcoholic. Winston had never talked about his job, but once, Barry had noticed an MI6 ID badge in Winston's hand while he rummaged through his briefcase looking for his wallet. Barry had never said a word about it.

Barry could tell from Christie's voice that he wasn't talking to a mere neighbour or relative about Winston's plight. There was too much power behind her voice. An effortless authority.

'I'm sorry to bother you with this–' Barry spluttered.

Christie cut him off. 'Don't worry. You did the right thing. I'll deal with this now.' Before she left, Christie added, 'Oh, and Barry? Delete this number from your phone now.'

Without waiting for a response, Christie hung up, then removed the SIM card from the burner, and tossed both into her microwave in the kitchen and let it sizzle and spark for a minute until both were destroyed.

She marched back to the hall and phoned her driver. 'I need you to come back. I'm not done for the night, it would seem.'

CHAPTER FIVE

Cambridge Street, Pimlico, London

Olivia Christie's driver was grateful for the SatNav guiding him through the streets of Pimlico, as every street looked the same. The white stucco terraces, pillars at the front steps, over-hanging balconies. The architecture favoured by foreign consulates in the city, except a little more ragged around the edges.

'Wait here,' Christie told the driver. If Winston was a drunken mess, she didn't want anyone else to see it.

She hurried up Winston's front steps, and into his building using the spare key he had given her months ago when she agreed to be his sponsor. She kept her phone in her hand, ready to call Winston if the door had been locked or chained from the inside. She had no idea what she was walking into, but if Winston had started drinking again then it was likely he would want to shut out the outside world.

Indeed, when Christie slotted her key into Winston's front

door on the second floor, the door opened a few inches, then a chain on the inside pulled taut.

Christie sighed, then called through the gap in the door, 'Leo, it's Olivia.' Recoiling at how loudly her voice was booming through the otherwise silent staircase, she lowered her voice. 'I'm not angry,' she explained. 'I just want to talk.' She paused, waiting for an answer that didn't come. She sighed again, then called Winston's mobile.

It rang out.

Directing her voice into the house again, she said, 'Leo... Leo, we have to talk...'

One of Winston's neighbours across the landing opened her door, ready to let loose a volley of complaints that this wasn't the kind of building to tolerate disturbances at eleven on a Friday night.

Before the complaints could start, Christie instead appealed, 'Have you heard from Leo tonight?'

The neighbour replied, 'I heard him come back about half an hour ago. Is he all right?'

Christie peered in through the gap in the door again. On the street outside, a taxi was making a three-point turn, which threw its headlights momentarily across Leo's living room ceiling, casting a shadow of something in the living room towards the hall.

The moment Christie saw it, her movements turned frantic. She cried out, 'Oh my God...' She turned in profile towards the door, then thrust her full weight into the door. Preparing herself for another attempt, Christie told the neighbour, 'Call an ambulance!'

The neighbour ran back inside and called to someone in her flat.

Winston's door wouldn't give. Christie turned around,

looking for anything she could use to get the door open. Then she saw a fire extinguisher hanging on the wall on the landing above.

Christie dashed upstairs to get it. She swung it hard at the bottom of Winston's door, then again near the top. The dual impacts took the door off its hinges, giving Christie access to the flat – and the full horror of what was inside.

In the living room, Winston swung from a rope thrown over the chandelier in the centre of the ceiling. A chair lay grimly on its side underneath him, having been kicked away.

Winston's eyes were closed. He was out cold – not that he had been fighting it before he passed out. He had kicked the chair away with a sense of relief, that it was going to be over after a short passage of pain. The pain didn't matter. He had lived through much worse in his life already. Anyone who survives six months of torture and isolation at the hands of the brutal Chinese Ministry of State Security doesn't have much left to fear in this world.

An empty bottle of Jack Daniels sat on the coffee table. No music was playing. The TV off. Evidently, Leo wanted to take his own life in total silence. Like a dog who retreats under the stairs when he knows he's dying.

Christie ran to Winston, pulling the chair upright then standing on it herself to get up to his height. She hugged Winston around the thighs, to take the pressure off his neck that had been throttled by his bodyweight. 'Help!' Christie shouted. 'Living room! Help!'

The neighbour and her husband came running through, then stopped in the doorway, horrified by what they were seeing.

'Get a knife...' Christie groaned. 'Something...'

The husband ran to the kitchen and came back brandishing

a huge butcher knife. With a few curt lashes, he managed to cut the rope. But the damage – as far as Christie could tell – had already been done.

Winston was unresponsive to every slap and demand and plea to wake up.

As Christie began CPR, she snapped at the neighbour, 'How long for that ambulance?'

'They just said as soon as possible...'

'That's not quick enough.' Christie shook her head, then gestured at her phone, which she had dropped on the floor. 'Get into my phone. Dial zero zero hashtag and don't hang up.'

Confused, the neighbour did as Christie said. 'What should I say?'

'You don't have to say anything. It's an emergency code.'

'But...what about an address?'

'Trust me, there's no turning off location on that phone, and I'm not the sort of person who can go missing. An ambulance will be here in two minutes max.' Christie pressed hard up and down on Winston's chest. 'Come on, Leo, stay with me. Help's coming. You hear me? I've called it in. Stay with me...'

CHAPTER SIX

Isle of Skye, Scotland

GRANT HAD BEEN up all night, planning each move meticulously. Strategising every countermeasure, every contingency. Once he was done, he surveyed his living room wall where he had assembled the blueprint for his mission. The wall plastered with the material he had assembled over the previous weeks. Pictures and maps of an address marked as "1 Carlton Gardens" in central London, along with another address marked as "Chevening House" highlighted on an Ordnance Survey map of Kent in south east England. There were itineraries and timetables that Grant had no business having, but in the modern world with Grant's connections, there was no information that couldn't be had for a certain price, or for certain favours.

At the centre of it all was a photo of Gretchen Winter. A former Hannibal agent betrayed by her corrupt boss, Imogen Swann. When Swann was murdered by rogue Albion operative Henry Marlow, it left Gretchen in the wind. Trapped undercover with no way out. Swann had been burying Gretchen's reports for months, and had been the only one in the world who knew Gretchen was out there. A total ghost. Until Gretchen's attempts to warn MI6 about the imminent attack on foreign embassies around the world sent Grant on a mission to track her down.

Grant had pinned her photo to the wall as a reminder to himself of what all of this was about. A mission that could very well be his last.

He took down the pictures of the Crown Prince of Saudi Arabia Mohammad bin Abdul, and his corrupt business partner, Foreign Secretary, the Right Honourable John Wark. All that was left to do was pick up the holdall he had packed, slip on his navy baseball cap and brave the weather outside. It had turned sharply from clear skies overnight to rain and thunder at dawn.

It could do that on Skye. As well as in the heart of a covert operative with revenge on his mind, and nothing left to lose.

But as Grant collected his bag, he saw the faint glow of car headlights rising and falling, twisting and turning along the B road at the end of the long snaking driveway leading to his cottage. The progress of the headlights slowed as they approached the turn-off for Grant's driveway.

Grant stared at the black Range Rover, wondering whether to run or not. If they had come to kill him, he wouldn't have seen or heard a car. He would already be lying on the floor with a bullet in his head. Grant dropped his holdall and opened his front door.

Olivia Christie's driver stopped the car and she got out, bracing herself against the weather.

Wind and rain lashed against her, coming in hard off the coast. She had to raise her voice to be heard over the waves crashing against the rocks not far behind the cottage, and the howling wind.

'You're a hard man to find these days, Duncan.'

Grant leaned against the front door and folded his arms in a defensive posture. 'I doubt it took up a lot of MI6's resources to find me at the address that's listed on my personnel file.'

'This isn't the first time someone has come calling here.'

'I've been away.'

Christie shut her door and gestured towards the cottage. 'Making plans?'

Grant said nothing.

'I've known every step you've taken since you left Saudi airspace a month ago,' she said.

'Maybe not every step,' Grant replied. 'How did you know I was here?'

'Don't flatter yourself, Duncan. As much as we have people who know how to disappear, we have just as many who know how to find people like you.' Christie held her jacket collar up against the wind. 'This isn't exactly the warm welcome I was told to expect around here. Are you going to invite me in?'

Grant looked over his shoulder, thinking about what his living room looked like.

'If it's about me seeing whatever plans you've made, you needn't worry. I'm not here about that. I'm here with a warning.'

CHAPTER SEVEN

Grant made them both cups of coffee, then took them to the living room where Christie had been eyeing the photo of Gretchen on the wall.

'I've sometimes wondered what sort of place a man like you would live in,' Christie said.

'If you've got any suggestions for decor, I'm all ears. I don't get many visitors.'

Christie paused to consider how best to classify the spartan surroundings. There was no TV. No framed photos on tables. No paintings or pictures on any walls. 'It's like a monk's retreat has been burgled and the heating cut off.'

'Sounds about right,' said Grant, handing her a cup of steaming coffee. 'You look tired, ma'am. What's happened?'

Christie cradled the cup in her hands to warm them. The cottage was only marginally warmer than outside, minus the wind chill. 'A few weeks ago, we lost three Albion agents.'

'Albions?'

'*Former* Albion agents. Retired.'

'I don't know what surprises me more. The fact that there

were that many still around, or that someone went to the trouble of killing them. You're worried I'm next, is that it?'

Christie scoffed. 'That's right, Duncan. I took a flight to RAF Buchan in the middle of the night and drove a hundred miles because I was worried about your safety.'

'I don't understand,' said Grant. 'You want me to play detective and catch whoever did it?'

'I can't say any more about it here. Maybe if you hadn't gone dark across all communication channels, this would have been easier for us both.'

Grant didn't reply.

Christie leaned down to meet his eye line. 'You do know I could fire you for going AWOL, don't you? MI6 doesn't do self-catering, Duncan. You are an employee.'

Grant shook his head. 'Not for long. Fire me if you wish, but what I have to do is bigger than any job or salary.'

Christie paused. 'Why were you in Paris last week? Then Lahore? And Lake Tahoe a few days later?'

Grant didn't reply.

'I know you want to make them pay, Duncan,' Christie said. 'Hell, on any other week I might have asked to tag along. John Wark and the Crown Prince's day will come. That I promise you–'

Grant snorted and shook his head.

'You don't believe me?' she asked.

'I think it's a thin line between optimism and delusion.'

Christie waited a moment before warning him, 'Careful, Duncan. I've always liked you, but you don't get to call the Director of MI6 delusional.'

'Pardon me, ma'am,' he said, before doubling down. 'But it *is* delusional. The agency buried evidence that John Wark conspired with the Crown Prince to murder Kadir Rashid, who was on the cusp of exposing a crooked property deal that Wark brokered–'

Christie fired back, 'I buried that evidence to protect this agency. It got the Albion programme up and running again, with Leo in charge. I put you at the *centre* of its operations, Duncan.'

'And what good did it do?'

Christie knew he was right, but the pair of them weren't going to solve what was wrong with the agency over a cup of coffee in a cottage on Skye. 'Someone has been killing Albions, Duncan, and I need to find out why. These were professional hits. Now there's only two of you left.'

'Who's the other Albion?'

Christie thought about answering. 'I won't get into that. Not here. In a secure room.'

'I'm sorry the agency's lost personnel, but it's not my fight.'

'Take a look around, Duncan. The fight is on your doorstep whether you like it or not. I need you both to bring the other Albion in for his own protection.'

Grant did a double-take. 'Both?'

'I'm not sending you in alone on this. I'm not taking any chances. This is bigger than me or you or the Albion programme.'

'Who else are you sending in?'

'Someone you've worked with in the past. Though not for a while. Not since Kill School.'

Grant's eyes widened. 'You're sending me in with *Ridley?*'

'I've read the reports. I know what you two did at Kill School.'

Ridley. It had been a long time since Grant had heard the name. Kill School. Where MI6 turns agents into killers.

'And if I say no?' said Grant.

'Like I said,' Christie explained. 'This is bigger than you and me or the agency.'

'You didn't travel through the night to tell me about an op.'

Christie nodded slowly, with purpose. 'No. I didn't.'

'What's happened, ma'am? What aren't you telling me?'

'It's about Leo,' she said.

CHAPTER EIGHT

A mere two hours after their conversation in Grant's cottage, both Grant and Christie were in the air on a plane borrowed from the Foreign Office – just the latest in a long line of favours extracted from John Wark by Christie. Such were her demands, and so often were they met, that rumours had circled Westminster that either Wark and Christie were having an affair, or Christie had dug up dirt on the minister who also happened to be responsible for her agency.

Christie was at the front of the plane behind a soundproof and frosted glass door, fielding a conference call with Fifteen Flags directors across multiple international time zones.

Grant watched Christie's fuzzy silhouette striding around, as she went off on one of her monologues about the need for transparency between the countries that had formed an alliance to combat terrorism through a shared network of agents and black operations. Grant was in awe that one person could shoulder such responsibilities, taking it all in her stride. Just another day. Meanwhile, he was fighting back tears, thinking about what Leo had tried to do to himself.

Grant blamed himself. If he hadn't been running around the world planning vengeance, then he might have been in a position to help – or at least notice that Winston was struggling with something. It was impossible for him not to think of his own dad's alcoholic oblivion, and Grant's failure to stop him drinking himself to death. The reality was that Leo Winston had played a far more significant role in Grant's life than anyone else. He had plucked Grant out of SAS training, and thrust him into the high-octane world of international espionage. There was nothing Grant wouldn't do for Leo. Even if it meant holding off his planned mission to avenge Gretchen.

Seeing John Wark and Mohammad bin Abdul in handcuffs or in the ground would have to wait.

Grant told himself he had to remove any emotion from the situation. He wouldn't be at his best if he made emotional decisions. But piece by piece, the emotional bricks were stacking up like a wall in front of him. Now, on top of everything else, he had to go on an op with Ridley of all people.

And if past experience was anything to go by, it wouldn't be a straightforward op.

CHAPTER NINE

THREE YEARS AGO

Grant was ushered into a room that looked to him like a small university seminar room. A short, bald man strode around at the front of the class, dwarfed by a whiteboard that was metres long.

The other Section 7 recruits were already in their seats when Grant came in, all talking jovially and sharing jokes in such a way that made Grant feel like he had missed some sort of induction event or social gathering. How did they all seem to be on such familiar terms with each other?

Grant reminded himself he was probably being paranoid, but it felt like the SAS all over again. He had gone against the grain from day one there, too. Although, ironically, his single-mindedness and solitary nature were what had marked him out so clearly to his Directing Staff Mikey Forrester, who had recommended Grant to Leo Winston.

When Grant heard a rough Scottish accent booming from the front of the class, he relaxed a little more.

'Take your seats and button it,' the bald man snapped.

Instant silence.

'My name's Billy Reid and you're not going to like me,' he said, still speaking at the same volume as when he'd been fighting to be heard just a moment ago. 'I'm going to push you to places you don't want to go, and say things to you that you don't want to hear.' He paused. 'If you don't like that, you know where to go.' He pointed to the door.

Reid spent the next fifteen minutes explaining in detail what he was going to demand from them. And if anyone didn't think they were up to it, they should leave before the going got tough.

Incredibly, to Grant's way of thinking, two recruits actually walked. Put off by Reid's aggressive manner and the portentous, ominous assignments that were being discussed.

Reid didn't even attempt to mask what he thought of the two recruits throwing in the towel before the end of induction. 'Goodbye, ladies,' he told the two young men without looking at them. 'You won't be missed.'

The pair ruffled their long, thick hair, snorting contemptuously under their breath as they left the room.

'Anyone else?' Reid demanded.

No one else dared move.

'Good,' said Reid. 'What those two were probably scared of is that if you're successful in being admitted to Section 7, it's going to be the end of your current lives as you know it. It's going to demand sacrifices. Working towards something greater than your own ego. Your own wealth or happiness. This is about safeguarding the British people. Your fellow men and women. Can anyone think of a sacrifice more worthy than that?'

There were a few recruits who had some ideas, but they were too terrified to mention them.

'Good,' said Reid, then pointed at Grant. 'You.'

Grant felt a jolt of electricity fire through his body.

'Is there a reason you're sitting about two metres away from everyone else?'

Without hesitating, Grant said, 'There was a lot of talking when I came in. I didn't want to be distracted.'

Reid nodded sharply. 'Good point. Everyone, space out until you're at least an arm's length away from the person next to you. In case you haven't cottoned onto it yet, the other people in this room are not your friends. They're your competition.' Reid strode back and forth in front of the whiteboard, which was still empty. Then he stopped, picked up a black marker and wrote "94%" in the middle of the board, then he circled the number. 'That's the failure rate for applicants on this course. There are twenty-year veterans in MI6 who don't know what goes on at Section 7. For the six per cent of you who do make it through…you're going to be the sharp end of the stick. Operating with professionalism and executing your orders to the letter in some of the worst hellholes this planet has to offer.' Reid raised his head expectantly. 'Sound good?'

The collective response was unwavering. 'Yes, sir.'

While Reid concluded the induction, Grant began naming the recruits according to a pack of cards. He assigned each card a specific place in an imaginary mansion, pairing the card with a memorable object. So jack of spades would be paired with an ornament of a heron that reminded Grant of a certain recruit's long thin neck. And the queen of hearts would be paired with a cushion that had a large red heart sewn onto the front, that reminded Grant of the young woman whose constant smile and evident happiness marked her out to him as an almost certain course-failure. On and on Grant went, assigning each recruit a card and an accompanying object.

He even assigned himself a card: the jack of clubs – a card no one really cares about or notices.

Then, there's always a Joker in the pack. One that you can't quite figure out. One who's staunchly himself, yet still part of the pack.

There was only one candidate for that card, as far as Grant saw it.

They called him Ridley.

CHAPTER TEN

EIGHT WEEKS LATER

PICCADILLY, LONDON – RUSH HOUR

Senior Instructor Billy Reid managed not to show it, but he knew he was being followed. Since Bond Street at least. Maybe earlier.

He didn't panic. He couldn't afford to. He was far too experienced for that. When you've run several high-profile snatch-and-grabs from Helmand to Helsinki, and renditioned terror suspects on four different continents, having a tail in a major capital city with plenty of outs, a radio in your ear, and carrying a concealed Glock, felt like just another work day.

The tail was certainly good.

Reid made a sudden left, down into Piccadilly Underground where he was met with a tsunami of morning commuters. On a Monday morning, a stop like Piccadilly was almost ninety per cent a destination rather than a departure point.

He had to pick his way deftly through the crowd, taking a few hits to the shoulder from people lost to their phone screens.

Put your bloody phone away and watch where you're going, he thought.

It was no wonder sweaty, nervy terror suspects could move around cities so easily. Absolutely no one was paying any attention.

The crowd had slowed his progress, enough for the tail to now be within fifty yards of him. But in Piccadilly Underground that could have been a mile away.

He pushed on and said loud enough to be heard, 'Police... move, please...'

That was all it took for the commuters to part like the Red Sea.

Although he wasn't a police officer, as an instructor on the Secret Intelligence Service's elite Section 7 programme, he granted himself whatever latitude he required in order to stump a recruit on their final training run. Even if that meant impersonating a police officer. After all, none of the terrorists and gangsters and gun-runners and drug dealers the recruits would face in the real world played by any kind of rules either.

Once Reid had crossed the packed concourse by the turnstiles, he dashed up the stairs leading back to Piccadilly Circus.

Another shoulder-check confirmed it: his tail was still there.

He got on the radio. 'Who did you say my tail was?'

'Duncan Grant,' came the reply in his ear.

After a pause, Reid replied, 'I should have known. He's not bad.'

Monitoring the radio in an unmarked van off the tight lane of Air Street, European Task Chief Officer Leo Winston gave a faint smile. 'That's the most glowing praise Billy Reid's ever given a Section 7 candidate.'

Next to him, Winston's deputy Miles Archer remarked,

'He's got a point, though, boss. I can't remember anyone sweeping through Kill School the way Grant has.'

Winston's smile disappeared. 'I really wish people would stop calling it that.'

Reid had suspected it was Grant. None of the other candidates had thrust themselves to the front of the pack like Grant. Apart from maybe Ridley.

As far as Reid was concerned, everyone else was playing for consolation prizes compared to Grant and Ridley. The others had distinguished themselves. But Grant and Ridley had been so good, Reid couldn't face having anyone else join them in graduation. Compared to Grant and Ridley, the others were leagues behind. They weren't even playing the same sport. It was Connect Four versus three-dimensional chess.

On street ops, Grant had left a team of five running in circles around Hyde Park. Ridley had manipulated two female candidates since day two of training, using his considerable armoury of charm and Hugh Grant-level of foppish good looks to play them off each other, before viciously betraying them both in a team exercise where both women believed they had partnered with Ridley on the exercise.

'It's not personal,' he had explained to them. 'But the fact is, if you were both cut out for Section 7, you'd have seen it coming a mile off.'

It had been drilled into Grant growing up that no one likes the smartest kid in the class. But the smartest kid in class who also happens to be the most handsome, as well as being great at sports, along with affable and witty, tends to do quite well. Ridley had been that sort of kid. Graduating Kill School was just another in a long line of achievements. Where the road ended for someone like him was anyone's guess. Winston figured Ridley for at least a section chief by the time he was thirty-five – which would have made him the youngest section chief in agency history.

As for Grant? Winston couldn't imagine him anywhere other than in the field. Living in the shadows. Close to no one. Living only for the job.

'Where's he gone?' asked Reid.

'I don't have eyes,' Winston responded.

Reid kept moving, but looked all around. Grant was nowhere to be seen.

Then, out of nowhere, Ridley laid a hand on Reid's shoulder and told him, 'He's broken off.'

Reid ran to catch up as Ridley set off in pursuit of Grant.

Both Reid and Ridley were side by side now. Each with the shared goal of keeping Grant at bay.

'What do you mean he's broken off?' asked Reid. 'He's an hour from completing his final training op.'

'So am I,' Ridley retorted, the annoyance in his voice obvious.

Then, breaking all protocols, Grant joined the men over the radio. 'We've got a problem here,' he said.

'Does he think he's in a movie or something?' said Ridley, then did a mocking impression of his rough Hebridean accent.

Reid didn't find it amusing. 'Grant wouldn't trail off over nothing.'

'The prick's about to cost me my final training op completion. I don't pass without him finishing as well, do I?'

Winston reminded Ridley of the rules. 'You're not getting admitted into Section 7 without demonstrating you can shake an adequate tail, Ridley.'

Reid's eyes were everywhere. Hunting. Hungry. Still, he was able to converse with Ridley. 'There's no graduation by default in this course, young man.'

Ridley scowled under his breath, then he got on the radio. 'Grant, you're about to cost me completion, you silly prick. Come back on course and finish this.'

'I can't do that,' Grant replied. He sounded like he was running now. 'I'm in pursuit...' His voice was shaking with increasing intensity. 'I've got a terror suspect in sight.'

'Oh, don't be stupid,' Ridley whined.

Reid was the only one to take it seriously. 'What have you got Grant?'

'Male, Middle Eastern, twenty to twenty-five...' There were dozens of data points that Grant could have given them, but it all came down to one overarching thing. 'He's just not right. The whole picture.'

Winston cut in. 'Billy, I've had word from Thames House. It seems that Five had a man in play this morning. Their man just lost him on the underground.'

Reid was running now. 'Description!'

Winston gave it.

'It's him!' Grant assured them all.

Five minutes later, he was on an out-of-service platform at Piccadilly Circus, straddling a terror suspect who had a ten-inch butcher's knife hidden down his trouser leg.

While the station was being evacuated, Reid and Ridley sprinted towards the fray. They were both gasping for breath by the time they caught up to Grant. Counter Terror Firearms Officers had the scene surrounded within minutes, weapons drawn. Grant disarmed the man safely, then allowed the police to take over. It took Billy Reid quite a lot of convincing to explain to SCO19 who they were, and what they were up to.

'Your recruit's just stopped a major terror attack,' the senior officer at the scene explained to Reid and Ridley.

Ridley scoffed. 'How the hell did Grant know that?'

The senior officer showed Ridley an evidence bag with a mobile phone in it. 'The suspect had a live maps function running on the phone. The destination was Trafalgar Square.'

'Yeah,' said Ridley, 'because God knows, no one who looks of Middle Eastern-descent has any interest in visiting a major tourist landmark like Trafalgar Square.'

The officer then produced bag number two. A ten-inch butcher's knife, with Arabic writing down the blade. 'In case you're wondering, that translates as "there is only glory in jihad for the sake of God." Still on the fence that Duncan hasn't stopped a major terror attack?'

Grant walked behind them as if nothing had happened.

'Hey,' Ridley called to him. 'You just cost me completion, you showboating prick.'

Reid pulled Ridley away. 'And you've just shown me exactly the sort of operative you'd be in the field, Ridley. Go home. We'll go again after we've debriefed.'

Ridley made a point of connecting with Grant's shoulder on the way past – though he didn't move Grant nearly as much as he would have liked.

'That was a hell of a job, Duncan,' Reid told him. 'How did you know?'

Grant shook his head. 'I saw him on the Tube. It's like I said...he wasn't right. Everything. He had this robotic walk. But it wasn't like a limp. Then there was nervy demeanour and sweating.' Grant indicated their surroundings. 'It's freezing today, and he wasn't overdressed. He was fidgeting with his hands. Everyone seems calm delivering a monologue about jihad to a static camera. But strap a knife to your leg and walk through central London, and you'll see what someone's really made of. He's an amateur. But he's not harmless.'

Reid patted him on the back, once and firmly.

'Don't congratulate me too much,' said Grant. 'I failed completion as much as Ridley.'

Reid looked over his shoulder, noticing someone joining them. 'I was going to talk about that with a colleague of mine.'

Grant looked around and saw a man he hadn't seen since SAS training. A man who had looked curiously out of place at the time. The only man wearing a suit on the Brecon Beacons that day.

'Leo Winston,' he said, holding out his hand. 'European Task Chief. I'd like to talk to you about a job.'

Grant was still watching Ridley in the distance.

'Forget about him,' Winston told him. 'You're never going to see him again. Where you're heading, he's not.'

CHAPTER ELEVEN

Winston had been taken to St Thomas' Hospital in the heart of Westminster – the same hospital where the British Prime Minister would be taken in an emergency. He had a private room arranged by Olivia Christie on grounds of security. Winston had been in and out of consciousness since arriving at the hospital.

When Christie got him breathing again on the floor of his flat, he was too groggy to make any sense. The circumstances that she found Winston in didn't appear suspicious in any way, but she wasn't going to take any chances. A police officer had been assigned to the corridor outside his room to be sure.

Ordinarily, Grant would have taken the opportunity to get some sleep. Winston could have been out for hours given the meds he was on, and with the police officer outside, there was no need for Grant to be on his guard. But he couldn't sleep.

He couldn't get out of his head how much pain Winston must have been in to attempt such a thing.

A white bandage had been wrapped around Winston's neck, which had been treated for serious rope burns and abrasions. Other than a very pale complexion, Winston looked in otherwise fine shape. But what had been going through his mind the night before, that would take a lot longer to figure out and treat.

It made Grant think about how fragile a human head really is. Other than some flesh and bone, all that keeps a human head on a body is gravity. It takes surprisingly little force to remove a head from a body. Of course, cutting through a neck is grisly, messy work. But as far as explosive force required to remove a head, it doesn't take much.

Grant had plenty of time to think about what he might say to Winston when he woke up – the doctors had assured Grant and Christie that it was a matter of when, not if. But when Winston's eyes fluttered, and he let out a series of low frequency groans, Grant found himself tongue tied.

He crouched next to Winston's bed, holding his hand. 'Hey, it's all right. It's me, Leo. It's Duncan.'

Winston croaked, 'How long have I been out?'

'Most of the night. You were coming in and out a few hours ago.'

The realisation that he was still alive then hit Winston like a lorry slamming into a brick wall.

'Fuck...' He lifted his arms, then dropped them impotently down on his lap.

'Yeah,' said Grant. 'Still here.'

'Fuck...I'm sorry, Duncan.'

'You don't have to say sorry.'

'I was going to call you. But...Where were you?'

'What do you mean? Last night?'

'You know what I mean.'

Grant paused. 'We shouldn't do this now. You need to rest.'

'Where were you?' Winston insisted.

'I was working.'

'Bollocks. Not officially you weren't. Christie knows you've been travelling under assumed names.'

Grant didn't bother to deny it.

'Grant Winter?' said Winston with a wry chuckle. 'I didn't figure you for the sentimental type.'

'And I didn't figure you for the…' He broke off.

'What?' Winston asked. 'Weak type?'

'That's not what I was going to say.'

'It's what you *meant* to say.'

'We owe it to each other to stick around and finish this thing.'

'What thing?'

'To bring John Wark and the Crown Prince to justice.'

Winston sighed and looked to the ceiling. 'I can't believe this is the first conversation I'm having after waking up.'

'Am I wrong?' Grant asked.

'I ran out of fight, okay?'

'Why? What changed?'

'Come back to me when you're twenty years in and you'll know all about it.'

Grant pulled gently on Winston's hand for emphasis. 'Hey. You *never* give up, Leo. No matter what life throws at you. You never *ever* give up.'

Winston couldn't look at him. 'I didn't give up, Duncan. I fought. Every day since I got back from China. I did everything I could to not drink. But I was in just as much pain every day as when I was drinking. I thought…what's the point? I might as well give myself the relief for once.' Winston finally locked eyes with Grant. 'They were going to suspend me. Over Marlow. The agency money that you nearly lost–'

'We got it back.'

For the first time, Winston raised his voice. 'Yeah, but you didn't know that you could get it back when you shot Henry Marlow in the head, Duncan!'

Grant didn't have a defence.

Winston went on, 'You disappeared and I was left to clean up the mess. The job was all I had, and I thought they might take it away from me. So I had a drink…and that was all it took for the sky to fall down. Because I can't have just one drink. I need a hundred drinks.'

'I know,' Grant relented. 'I get it.'

'What you need to get, Duncan, is that the Foreign Secretary is gunning for you. He wants your head. The money was still in play when you shot Marlow. That would have been his career. Do you think he's not eyeing up the top job? Everyone figures him for Downing Street after the next election.'

'That's why I have to stop him before he gets a chance.'

'Why? Why does it matter?'

'Because I won't let him get away with it.'

Winston fired back, 'That's what they *do*! Don't you get that yet? They always get away with it, Duncan. These guys, they walk between the raindrops. Nothing ever lands on them.'

'Christie's asked me to come back for a job.'

'What sort of job?'

'Someone's killing former Albions.'

'She sending just you?'

'Me and a guy I knew at Kill School called Ridley.'

Winston pushed his lips out. 'Don't know him. But I'll tell you, if you're smart, you'll walk away from all of this while you still can.'

Grant squinted. 'What are you talking about? Walk away. From what?'

'Everything,' said Winston. 'Wark. Abdul. The agency.

Everything. While you still can. In fact, I don't think you should walk. I think you should run.'

Grant shook his head slowly in confusion. 'Leo, what else happened last night? Something changed.'

Ignoring the question, Winston said, 'We can't win, Duncan. The good guys. We can't win.'

'I don't believe that,' Grant replied. 'I won't believe that. I *can't* believe that.'

'Well, maybe you should.'

Grant stood up, preparing to leave.

'Duncan,' Winston began. 'I told you once that the lesson in this game isn't trust no one. The lesson is trust me.'

'I remember,' Grant replied. 'Why are you telling me now?'

'Because I'm asking you to trust me now. Get out. While you still can.'

'I've got a briefing at Vauxhall Cross.' Grant opened the door. 'Get some rest, Leo. You need to get your strength back.'

CHAPTER TWELVE

THE BRIEFING HAD BEEN SET for the Sensitive Compartmented Information Facility – or 'skiff', otherwise known as the 'Tank' – on the tenth floor. Designed for the most sensitive of discussions and briefings, the SCIF was a secure room that was insulated from any kind of electronic surveillance, or audio, visual or electrical penetration.

When Grant had first encountered it, it looked like someone had left a shipping container in one of the disused conference rooms. It had, in fact, been built from scratch in the room by contractors with 'Secret' or above security clearance for government contract work.

The inside of the Tank wasn't exactly comfortable. A few basic office chairs and a conference table, with whiteboards on the wall, and a basic MI6 mainframe computer set-up. It wasn't just the decor that was uncomfortable. Inside the Tank, Grant and Ridley sat on opposite sides of the conference table across from each other. A lengthy and tense silence had stretched out since Ridley had come in, with neither man willing to back down first and break the silence.

Outside the Tank, Olivia Christie watched a feed on her phone from a camera inside the Tank, showing the ongoing standoff between the two men. Next to her was the agency's top forensics and tech expert, Randall.

'Ma'am,' said Randall nervously, 'I'm not entirely sure what you'd like me to contribute here.'

'I need someone I can trust to help these two in tracking down Robert Faraday.'

'It's just, I've got a lot of lab work to catch up–'

Christie looked up quickly from her phone, holding Randall's gaze in a way that sent a chill up his back. 'Randall,' she explained, 'Leo's in hospital, and Miles, God rest his soul, is no longer with us. Things have changed. We're all working out of our comfort zones on this one. Grant likes you. He trusts you. So I want you around.'

'Is Leo going to be okay, ma'am?' Randall asked.

Christie looked back at her phone.

Randall went on, 'It's just...Leo seemed a little off this past week.'

'He's been worried about Duncan. We all were. For now, I want you in there to get a handle on how bad things are between those two. God knows I would put anyone else in the world on a team with Grant, but they're the best individuals I have, and I can't farm this op out to anyone else in the agency. The Albion programme is still a secret known only to select people like yourself.' She paused, then looked at him expectantly.

Randall pointed towards the Tank door. 'Oh, should I... Okay, I'll go in.'

The tension in the air was evident the moment Randall entered the Tank.

'Oh, thank God,' Ridley announced. 'It's Jeeves.'

Grant fired daggers from his eyes at Ridley. 'His name's Randall. And he's got an IQ of about a hundred and sixty. You might want to listen to him.'

Randall pulled out a chair, sitting as far away from the men as he could. If he'd been any further away, he would have been back out in the conference room again.

'What exactly is your role here?' asked Ridley.

'Oh, I'm forensics and tech,' Randall answered.

Ridley narrowed his eyes. 'And why do we need forensics? We haven't even been briefed yet.'

'Is she coming?' Grant asked.

'Soon,' Randall replied, enjoying being able to indulge in even a white lie in the presence of the agency's two foremost operatives.

When another tense silence fell across the room, Randall shuffled nervously in his seat, trying to think of a question that might help Christie with some insights. 'So you two came up together in training?'

'Not necessarily at the same level,' said Grant.

'No,' Ridley added. 'Different levels, Randall. I followed procedure and protocol, while Grant did whatever the hell he liked, whether it left a trail of collateral damage in the process or not. But class always shines through in the end. I've been running in Section 7 for the past year now.' Ridley waited for Grant to weigh in.

Grant just stared at him. There was something about the way Ridley carried himself, the way he spoke, his entire nature, that annoyed him. When he talked about himself, Ridley had a way of sounding incredibly impressed with his own achievements.

'And what about you, Duncan?' asked Ridley. 'What adventures have you been up to? Our man in the Hebrides.'

Grant sat back in his chair, completely at ease. 'It's classified.'

Ridley said, 'Oooh,' with a smile. 'How impressive. What, is the first rule of Albion club that you don't ever talk about Albion club?'

Randall didn't know where to look. Or what to say. He left it to Grant.

'It's classified,' Grant repeated. 'And I don't know that you have the clearance for it.'

'I didn't need any clearance to hear about that mess you made in Lyon. Had half the French police hunting for you. Caused a shootout at an outdoor opera, is what I read. You know, in the international papers. It was in all of them.'

'You can't believe everything you read,' Grant said, then winked.

Ridley's smile and lighthearted demeanour suddenly vanished. 'I'll tell you this, old boy. Just don't get in my way out there, okay? In Section 7, we actually have to answer for our actions. Not just cause indiscriminate mayhem, then go on the run...'

Outside, Christie had heard enough. 'Right,' she said, acting as if she knew nothing of what had been going on. 'Are we ready to get to work?'

CHAPTER THIRTEEN

Christie pushed two copies of the same briefing report first to Grant, and then one to Ridley. She clasped her hands together. 'What you have in front of you, only two of my most trusted analysts and I have seen.'

Grant and Ridley opened the manila A4 envelopes and skimmed through the dossiers. There were no pictures. Only names neither man knew, and no obvious connective tissue between the names or locations mentioned.

'I don't understand,' said Ridley, still flicking through the dossiers. 'These are ordinary citizens.'

Grant flicked back and forth between the dossiers. Ridley wasn't the only one confused. There was a lot that didn't add up to Grant, even though Christie had already given him a head start by telling him the deceased had been Albion operatives.

'Look again,' said Christie.

Ridley couldn't understand what was so obvious, but didn't want Grant to figure out the answer first. Petulantly, Ridley shut the dossier, like a young boy taking his football home so no one else could play with it. 'They read like assassinations,' Ridley said. 'So what's the common denominator?'

Christie said, 'They were all retired Albion operatives.'

Ridley leaned back in surprise, then scoffed. 'That's been kept very quiet.'

'We are actually still responsible for quite a lot of secrets around here, Ridley.'

Grant held up the dossier on the first page. 'Sheila Hayworth is listed as seventy-six years old.'

'That's right,' Christie said.

Grant and Ridley exchanged a baffled look.

Ridley said, 'But I thought Albion only went back to the early two thousands. Hayworth was operational decades ago.' He turned to Grant again, then back to Christie. 'And I can tell by Scottish Daniel Craig over here's expression that he thought the same.'

Christie leaned forward on the table. 'What I'm about to tell you has been a STRAP Four classified secret kept by each of my predecessors. Several Foreign Secretaries have come and gone without ever knowing of its existence.'

Grant and Ridley waited with bated breath.

'The Albion programme goes back to the Cold War,' Christie admitted. 'Sheila Hayworth was in the field in nineteen eighty-two.'

'Where?' asked Grant.

Christie hesitated.

'If you want us to figure out who did this, ma'am, then we need to have a history of these operatives.'

'That's not on the table,' she said. 'I'm sorry. It can't happen. Not yet, anyway.'

Ridley added, 'Ma'am, it's not like me to agree with much Grant has to say, but if we don't know if these people were in

Moscow or Macclesfield, we've got little to go on as far as figuring out motive goes.'

'I'm not interested in finding out motives,' Christie said. 'I just want them stopped, and the last Albion secured.'

'You mean me?' asked Grant.

'Forgive me, Grant. I meant the last Albion before you. There's now only two Albions left, active or retired.' She slid across a further dossier. This one with a picture.

It showed a man's personnel photo. He had a sharp jawline, narrow eyes, and the smart side-parting of a businessman. There was nothing about him that suggested a man with any kind of military or special ops training.

'Looks pretty unremarkable,' said Ridley.

Christie replied, 'Then that would make you a terrible judge of character. His name's Robert Faraday. And believe me when I tell you that he was utterly exceptional.'

'Well, he's still alive,' said Grant, 'so that tells me something about how good he was.'

'How many Albions have there been?' asked Ridley.

'That's classified,' Christie answered. 'I can tell you that we lost a lot of them in the field, as you would expect. Henry Marlow took care of far more than I care to remember when we sent them off to capture or kill him. The others got out and retired. Some adjusted to life on the outside better than others. Some, like Sheila Hayworth, did the job and were able to move on and carve out a decent retirement for themselves. Others like James Docherty failed to adjust and lost themselves in drink or drugs. Yes, we lost a fair amount in the field, but we've also lost plenty to natural causes once they got out.'

'I'm just amazed you managed to bring the programme back,' said Ridley.

'I brought it back because of what Grant proved in

capturing Henry Marlow, and exposing Imogen Swann's treason. We need operatives like Grant in play. To do the things that politicians are unwilling to sanction even in private.'

'The question is,' said Grant, 'why kill them now?'

'Revenge, surely,' Ridley suggested. 'God knows whose feathers these guys ruffled over the years.' He flashed his eyebrows up at Christie, revelling in the opportunity to be a part of the Director's inner circle. 'Am I right?'

Christie demurred.

Grant kept flicking through the dossiers, looking for answers. 'Consistent methodology in the murders. Professional hits the lot of them.'

Ridley added, 'Not concerned about making them look like accidents.'

'No,' said Christie. 'Whoever did this wanted us to know.'

'But then, what's the threat?' asked Grant. 'Has there been any other communication? Any demands made?'

'Nothing,' Christie said.

'It can't be to silence someone. These three went out of their way to disappear back into normal everyday life. No suggestion of having one foot out of bed, and another still in it.'

'They must have still been active in some way,' said Ridley. 'What about the private sector?'

Christie shook her head. 'There's no evidence of that.'

'Nah,' said Grant. 'These guys were as out as out can be.'

'Sending a message?' Ridley wondered.

'What's the message?'

'I don't know, Grant. We're sitting here with less information than you get in a game of Cluedo. All we've got is speculation.'

Grant held up his report. 'These three were killed within a

few days of each other. That was weeks ago. If the plan is to go after Faraday next, what's taken them so long?'

Ridley added, 'What if Faraday's not even under threat? What if you're wrong, and there's something else going on?'

Grant peered at Christie. He knew when someone was withholding. 'What aren't you telling us, ma'am?' he asked.

Christie sighed. 'I think he might know something.'

'Is this an extraction or a rendition? Do you want us to save him or take him into custody?'

She paused. 'I don't know yet. All I know is that if anyone can shed light on what these murders are about, it's Robert Faraday.'

'I don't understand,' said Grant. 'Why can't we just contact him, warn him?'

'Send him a bloody email!' suggested Ridley, only half joking,

Christie said, 'Faraday didn't exactly leave the agency on the best of terms. I doubt there's a phone call from us that he would take.'

'Where's the extraction point?'

'Well off the grid. The far north of Scotland in Sutherland.'

'Sutherland?' Grant said in surprise.

'Where is that?' asked Ridley.

'It's the emptiest stretch of land in the country. If you want to disappear, that's the place to go.'

Christie said, 'Faraday's been living in the Matrix since he retired. No phone that we know of. No online presence. Completely self-sustained.'

'Are you expecting any resistance out there?'

Christie said, 'Beyond Faraday himself? I doubt it. But there could be hostile forces on their way to him as we speak.

Hell, we could get you up there and he's dead already. We won't know until you two walk in the door.'

'What if he refuses to come with us?'

Christie snorted, amused. 'Convince him.'

'He's an Albion, ma'am. He's taught to trust no one. And you said he's got a difficult relationship with the agency, and he doesn't know us. This could be tricky.'

Ridley gestured dismissively at the dossier. 'He might have been hot shit when he was in his thirties, but he's an old man, for god's sake.'

Grant pointed out with incredulity, 'He's fifty-five, Ridley.'

'Exactly. An old man.'

'It's a mistake to underestimate this guy.' Grant turned to Christie. 'Have you considered that he may be behind these killings?'

Christie nodded. 'Yes. But there's nothing in our intelligence network to indicate Robert Faraday wants anything to do with the outside world whatsoever. Let alone come out of retirement to commit multiple murders. It's a simple extraction. Bring him in safely, tuck him into bed in a safe house so we can get to the bottom of what these killings are actually about. Before you end up the last Albion, Grant.'

Randall, who had been sitting tensely, terrified to look anyone in the eye, got the nod from Christie. He handed over the intel they had gathered on Faraday.

Christie said, 'This is everything we have on his last-known location. I've got a plane ready to take you up north.'

'Inverness again?' asked Grant.

'The two of you will be flown to RAF Buchan in Aberdeenshire. From there, by car the rest of the way. You'll be on your own. Bring Faraday back to Buchan for debriefing. If we're lucky, it won't be too late.'

'And if we're too late?' Grant asked.

Ridley smirked. 'Then it's you on the chopping block next.'

Christie ignored the barb, directing only to Grant. 'Don't be late. You can follow up with me once you have him. I have to field questions from an emergency Foreign Select Committee hearing on why one of my operatives risked losing billions in MI6 slush funds during an operation. Should I mention your name or not, Duncan?'

Grant stared back sheepishly. 'Perhaps not,' he said.

'No,' Christie smiled. 'I thought not.'

Ridley looked at Grant in shock. For the first time since they'd known each other, he seemed genuinely impressed by Grant. Once Christie was gone, Ridley asked him, 'You really did that?'

Grant said, 'It was a little more complicated than she made it sound…but yeah.'

Walking past with the cocky stride that Grant remembered, Ridley remarked, 'What the hell have you been doing since Kill School…'

CHAPTER FOURTEEN

Olivia Christie was no stranger to the Foreign and Commonwealth Office on King Charles Street, but even she was in the dark about where exactly the staffer was taking her to, two floors down.

'Dear boy,' Christie began, 'you must be mistaken. I'm the Director of MI6 and I'm here for the Foreign Affairs Select Committee hearing.'

The young man, who was all of twenty-three years old, kept his composure. 'I know who you are, ma'am, and where I have to deliver you.'

'*Deliver* me?'

'The Committee is already waiting, ma'am. Everything's in order.'

But as the lighting grew dimmer and dimmer along the corridor, Christie felt like nothing at all was in order.

The staffer stopped at a blue door. Just like the other dozen they had already walked past.

'This is it, ma'am,' the staffer said, then opened the door, revealing the Foreign Affairs Select Committee sitting at a long conference table in a windowless room.

The Foreign Secretary John Wark looked up towards the staffer. 'Thanks, Freddie,' then beckoned Christie inside.

Christie did a double-take when the door was locked behind her by one of Wark's closest aides. 'I'm sorry, I thought I was testifying at a committee, not staging a run-through for nuclear fallout.'

She was particularly confused as to why Wark was there, and at the head of the table as if he was chairing the meeting.

Christie said, taking a seat, 'It's my rather amateur understanding, John, that the Committee's purpose is to examine and hold to account the running of the FCO.'

'There's been a bit of a change of plan,' Wark explained. 'Due to the highly sensitive nature of a number of items on the agenda, it was decided to move proceedings to somewhere more private.'

'Committee hearings are a matter of public record,' Christie said.

'Not today,' said a high-ranking member.

Someone else piped up, 'It's not in anyone's interests to have a matter such as the theft of billions of pounds from an MI6 mainframe computer within Vauxhall Cross end up on the front page of the papers.'

Wark gestured to the members around the table. 'Think of this is an informal opportunity for full and frank discussion.'

Christie had been around the block long enough to know political euphemism when she heard it. Full and frank discussion meant that they were about to grill her and then tear her to shreds. And without any cameras or media around, they could be as nasty as they had always wanted to be, but had never been able to in the past. The Henry Marlow debacle had provided the opportunity the less supportive members of the committee had been waiting for.

Jack Sopley, the MP for Rochdale, was one of them. As diehard anti-establishment as they came in Westminster. If the entire MI6 budget could be reduced to the price of a used car, he would have voted for it. 'Ms Christie,' he began, consulting the notes he had stayed up until the early hours to fine tune. 'A shootout at an open-air opera in Lyon, France. A former MI6 operative teaming up with a Congolese war lord. The armed siege and abduction of said operative outside Vauxhall Cross, and in the process causing millions of pounds of criminal damage. The theft of *billions* from an illegal slush fund for black ops from inside MI6 headquarters. The blowing up of an oil field in Saudi Arabia...' He peeled his glasses off. 'Ms Christie, would it be fair to say that MI6 is no longer a covert organisation?'

Christie glared at John Wark, on the verge of combusting with anger at him.

CHAPTER FIFTEEN

THE QUESTIONING only got harder and Christie's answers more defensive as one hour turned into two.

By this time, Christie had wrestled out of her suit jacket, cooking – as everyone else was – in the ventilation-free meeting room.

Another MP, Anne Vickers, was finishing up her round of questions. 'Can you assure us, then, Ms Christie, that MI6 has seen the last of its traitors? Because it seems to me that this...' She flicked back a page in her notes to check the name, 'these so-called Hannibal agents appear to be some of the worst offenders when it comes to committing treason and engaging in corruption. The very people you as director employed to clean up the agency's act.'

Christie might have been feeling the heat, but she had so far handled everything that had been thrown at her. Now she was close to the end, she wasn't about to falter. 'That's why,' Christie explained, 'the Hannibals are dead. I have axed the entire Anticorruption department.'

'Is that wise?' Vickers asked.

Christie retorted, 'You can ask for the department to be held accountable, or you can ask for it to be strengthened, but you cannot ask for both at the same time.'

Wark smiled softly to himself.

Christie continued, 'I'm taking over the running of all Anti-corruption department investigations. The entire concept of it needs a complete overhaul.'

'And you're the one best placed to do that, are you?'

Christie was unflappable. 'I am, yes.'

WHEN THE MEETING WAS OVER, Wark had to run to catch up with Christie, who had stormed out the moment the door had been unlocked.

'Olivia,' Wark called out, but she ignored him. 'Olivia,' he called louder.

She looked over her shoulder, but continued her brisk pace.

Wark finally caught up to her. 'Olivia, I'm sorry. I didn't have time to warn you. The fucking PM threw that together at the last minute.'

'I thought that it smelled like his work,' Christie replied. 'Didn't even have the guts to sit there and put those insulting questions to my face. Instead, he sends in goons like Anne bloody Vickers to throw shit on his behalf. He's a fucking estate agent with a side-parting. His every public utterance sounds like it was spat out by ChatGPT from the prompt "write me a speech that's the political equivalent of Laura Ashley." He should be on the board of a supermarket chain, or a hedge fund, trying to turn a quid fifty into a quid fifty-five, not running the country. God help me, but we used to have serious people in charge of things. Now it's like we've handed over power to a bunch of supply teachers.'

'You don't have to tell me,' Wark replied. 'I have to sit in his Cabinet meetings. And, God help me, every six weeks or so, I have to play golf with the fucker, then spend the evening looking at his weirdly square face over dinner.'

With the corridor to themselves, and anyone else far away, Christie stopped walking. 'You know as well as I do, John, that he's going to gut my budget come the spring. I can't have it.'

'Don't worry about him,' Wark said. 'I'm making some moves.'

'Then make them quickly. I've got an agency that's held together by string.'

Wark looked back towards the others far down the corridor. 'I'm more concerned about the dead Albions that have been washing up on various local newspapers in the past few weeks.'

Christie tried not to react.

'Oh yes,' said Wark, 'I know all about that. Now, if me and a couple of my guys can put together who they were, what's stopping someone in Fifteen Flags?' He prodded his finger at her. 'And then, what's stopping them putting together the common denominator between them all?'

Christie shook her head. 'No one's going to do that.'

'Really? Not even Duncan Grant?'

She paused. 'What about him?'

'That's who you've sent to find Robert Faraday, isn't it?'

'How did you find out that?'

'Never you mind. But I know that you've chartered a flight to RAF Buchan.'

Christie looked away.

Wark said, 'You're trying to extract him, aren't you? Faraday.'

Christie sniffed. 'I'm entertaining options.'

'Do you need me to remind you how bad an idea that would be? Faraday's been out of the game for years. God knows what's happened to him in the interim.'

'I need him off the streets for his own safety.'

Wark retorted, 'I need him *silenced*.'

Christie paused, longer this time. 'Are you saying…'

Wark nodded. 'I think you know exactly what I'm saying.'

'I can't do that, John. Not to one of our own.'

'You didn't have a problem ordering it when it was Henry Marlow.'

'First of all, I never ordered Grant to shoot Marlow. And secondly, Marlow was a completely difference case. He was a known fugitive. Faraday's a retired operative.'

Wark scoffed. 'Oh, Olivia. I think we both know he's far more than just that. If he's got what I think he has, he could bring down the whole bloody house of cards.'

'I understand,' Christie said.

'Do you really though? As the only thing standing between you and a Prime Minister who wants to send you packing?'

'Seriously?'

'It was all I could do to stop him from firing you this morning, Olivia.' He leaned in. 'So we understand each other.'

It wasn't a question.

Wark went on, 'It's time to do what should have happened months ago, Olivia. It's time to shut things down.'

'What's that supposed to mean?'

'We need to stay professional about this. I know that you've come to be attached to Grant, as has Leo. But when a programme goes south, we don't spend months giving it mouth to mouth. We tie it up and we put it in a box.'

'Are you seriously talking about–'

Wark stepped in closer, a strain of urgency cutting through his voice now. 'I'm talking about saving what might remain of our careers and pensions. You had me over a barrel in bringing back Albion, but it was a mistake, Olivia. There's no tomorrow for either of us unless we handle this now.'

'Handle. Tie it up. Shut things down. These all mean the same thing. You're talking about killing Duncan Grant. No wonder you're in favour of that. He knows every crooked deal you made with the Crown Prince, and I buried it for you.'

'You buried it so that you could get Albion back up and running. I did what you asked me to, and now that it hasn't worked out you want more rope. Well, it's too late. You've had all the rope you're going to get. Wrap this up, or when I'm sitting in Downing Street within the hour, I'll be recommending to the Prime Minister that we try taking MI6 in a new direction. Starting at the top.'

'You wouldn't dare,' Christie said, but she didn't sound sure.

'You bet your life I would. I've worked too hard to get this far. Now that I'm this close,' he indicated a tiny gap between two fingers, 'to Downing Street, I'm not having some Jock army reject fuck it up.' He sighed. 'It's time to let go, Olivia.'

Christie looked down at the ground. 'What a bloody terrible decision to have to make.'

'In fairness, Olivia, you have no other choice.'

Still shaking her head, Christie said, 'I'll tie it up with a second team. Make it clean.'

'And silent.'

'There won't be any noise,' she assured him. 'Somewhere as remote as where Robert Faraday lives you don't hear screams.'

CHAPTER SIXTEEN

It was mid-afternoon when Grant and Ridley landed at a misty, wet RAF Buchan in Aberdeenshire – the north-east corner of Scotland. Although the Ministry of Defence had downgraded Buchan from a manned station to a remote radar station, it had been merely an exercise in name only. Secretly, RAF Buchan had been going through huge renovations and modernisation. From a distance – which was all anyone could ever see of Buchan – the site appeared to be little more than a series of small outhouses and what looked like a giant golf ball: the radar dome.

The downsizing and renaming of Buchan as a remote radar station achieved what the MOD wanted: for no one to notice that it was actually building a private landing strip for aircraft and investing millions into its radar technology.

What few staff had been retained at the site operated under the strictest classified procedures, with locals having little idea that they were in fact living near one of the most closely guarded secrets in the British military industrial establishment.

Ridley asked, 'Why did they send us through Lossiemouth?'

'Too visible,' said Grant. 'Too many boots on the ground. They can control paperwork and personnel here better.'

'So this is home,' Ridley remarked, staring disappointedly out the Cessna Citation Latitude jet.

Grant snorted derisively. 'You know Scotland's got five and a half million people in it. We don't all live in Glasgow or Edinburgh. I'm from Skye on the other side of the country.'

'Looks bleaker than I expected.'

'That's the north east for you. Less mountainous, fewer trees, and much emptier than the west. Where we're going, though, that's unlike anywhere else in the country.'

'Good or bad?'

Grant smirked. 'You'll see.'

The personnel on the ground treated them with a mix of wonder and fascination. They didn't get much traffic through RAF Buchan, but when they did, the passengers were often important. You didn't get to use Buchan if you weren't.

A dark green Range Rover was waiting for Grant and Ridley, stocked with everything they would need for the long drive west across to Inverness, then north up the A9 along the north-west coastline. There was medical supplies, clothing, and of course weapons.

Knowing the roads better, Grant decided to drive.

They were crossing the Dornoch Firth bridge – a low road cutting straight across the vast expanse of water that eventually met the North Sea – when Ridley said, 'Would it kill you to say something once in a while?'

'What would you like me to say?' Grant asked.

'You haven't said a word in...' he checked his watch, 'thirty-seven minutes.'

'I was under the impression we were on a classified security operation. I didn't realise this was some kind of road trip date.'

'It doesn't make you mysterious, you know. Not talking. It just makes you dull.'

'If you'd walked in my shoes for a while, Ridley, you'd realise that there are far worse things to be in this game than dull. If you want to be memorable, audition for a reality TV show. If you want to stay alive, be dull. Leo Winston taught me that.'

Ridley looked out his window. 'Who?'

'You never knew Leo Winston?'

Ridley pushed his lips out. 'No. Who was he?'

'Is,' Grant corrected him. 'My handler and section chief.'

'Wow,' Ridley yawned. 'Fascinating...Look, what are you expecting out there?'

Grant didn't have to think very long about the question. 'The possibility that we're getting played.'

'What makes you think that?'

'Someone's killing former Albions and no one knows why. Apparently. Faraday has either been too clever for whoever's behind it all, or he's involved and someone's allowed him to stay alive. Either way, we're starting on the back foot.'

'It's also two against one.'

'Which only matters if we're talking about a physical confrontation. The only thing we know for sure about Faraday is that he was a good-enough Albion to not get killed doing the job. Outnumbering him doesn't give us much of an advantage. It's a mistake to underestimate him.'

Ridley shook his head and tutted.

'What?' asked Grant.

'They really did a number on you, didn't they?'

Grant didn't care to ask him to elaborate. Ridley could see

the mental and emotional places Grant had been since they had last met – and they had clearly had a substantial impact. Grant was harder in the eyes now. Stonier. Tougher to read. All his innocent Hebridean character had been eroded. Now all that MI6 had left of him was bare rock. Unknowable. Impenetrable.

Ridley said, 'Back in Kill School you were so full of earnest reverence for the agency and its mission. Doing the right thing.'

'I still am.'

'You know when they say trust no one, it's not strictly true. At a certain point you *have* to trust someone.'

'I don't believe that.'

'Well you got into a car with me.'

Grant flashed him a knowing smile. 'Because I got into a car with you means nothing, mate.'

'You don't even trust me? Even now?'

Grant watched the road ahead. They were heading into heavier rain, the sky above almost completely black. He told Ridley, 'We'll see.'

CHAPTER SEVENTEEN

Mile by mile, the landscape opened up, becoming increasingly barren and exposed. Gone were the forests and busy A-roads. The trees thinned out, giving way to views to the horizon of vast stretches of empty land. It wasn't even being farmed. It was just empty.

As the men turned west into the heart of Sutherland – the northernmost tip of Scotland – there was much less traffic. They went nearly twenty miles without seeing another vehicle. Any time a small cottage came into view, both Grant and Ridley wondered aloud how anyone could live in such remote surroundings. They were nearly fifty miles from the nearest village, let alone a town or a city.

Grant said, 'If you have a medical emergency at home out here, you're as well just calling ahead to a funeral directors rather than calling nine nine nine.'

'I guess that's the way Robert Faraday wants it out here,' replied Ridley.

Grant had a look around from west to east. 'It's good tactically though. Hard to surprise someone in such wide-open space.'

Ridley countered, 'But that's also what makes it hard to get away.'

The A roads turned into B roads, and then single-track roads with passing places, winding up and over Highland glens.

Ridley noticed the ruins of old cottages dotted around every few miles. 'I can't believe people used to live out here in numbers.'

Grant said, 'The clearances drove people towards the coast. The crofters became fishermen instead. That's why the centre of Sutherland's so empty.'

The landscape might have been desolate, but there was something extraordinarily beautiful about its wildness. Remote lochs and mountains of the strangest shapes gave the place an eerie and alien appearance. A sea of peat bogs, heather, and rock.

The perfect place to go for a man who doesn't want to be found.

The pair followed the GPS coordinates to Faraday's property, a small cottage halfway along a single-track road next to Loch Naver.

How anyone had ever ended up building a property of any description there was a mystery. It was certainly an old building with the occasional modern flourish like security lights underneath the gutters. Other than that, it was a traditional crofter's cottage painted in white that looked like it had been refreshed in recent years.

'Not ideal,' said Grant, as they turned onto the narrow, bumpy road. 'No escape routes off the road.' He leaned down to his left for a view out Ridley's window.

The light was fading fast.

'Looks pretty steep,' Ridley remarked about the intimidating hillside.

'That's deep heather all the way up there too.'

'Is that bad?'

'Two places I never want to end up in a foot chase: the desert, and through heather. You'd disappear up to your waist in there.' Grant gestured to his right. 'Then there's the water on this side. Nothing but this road ahead and behind.'

They pulled up outside Faraday's cottage. A multi-hour car journey wasn't exactly the best preparation before an op that might end up physical. But the men didn't have any choice but to stretch out quickly, then get on with the job.

Once the sun had set, darkness quickly set in – a deep inky black that only happens in remote countryside.

Grant went first to the rear of the Range Rover and opened up a locked steel armoury box. He checked one of the two Glock pistols inside was loaded, then he holstered it inside his Arc'teryx LEAF Atom jacket – a jacket made for special forces, cut from weatherproof softshell material and elastane to aid with freedom of movement.

Ridley looked at Grant in surprise. 'You don't actually think he'll unload on us, do you?'

'That's not the point,' said Grant, walking past.

As they approached the cottage up a steep, winding driveway, Ridley said, 'Not exactly the high-octane job I was looking for with an Albion. Drive across the Highlands to knock on someone's door? Christie doesn't need the pair of us, she needs a couple of Jehovah's Witnesses.'

'Knock it off,' Grant warned with a whisper. 'It's game time.'

Ridley's arrogance and laid-back attitude concerned Grant. Ridley didn't seem worried in the slightest. Grant couldn't work out if it was typical Ridley arrogance, or whether he knew something Grant didn't.

'You want to sneak around to take a look first?' asked Ridley.

'No,' Grant replied. 'If he's here, I don't want to spook him.'

Grant knocked on Faraday's front door. 'Robert,' he called out.

Ridley strayed towards the side of the house and pointed towards a window. 'TV's on...' He peeked inside, hard left, then hard right. He shook his head at Grant. 'Can't see him.'

Grant knocked louder this time. 'Robert, we're with SIS. We have concerns for your safety. We're coming in.'

Ridley followed closely behind, keeping an arm reaching back towards his own holstered Glock in case the worst should happen.

Walking slowly and carefully through the hall at the front door, the gentle sound of golf commentary from the TV came from the living room, a nagging distraction to Grant. If the TV was on, then where was Faraday?

Grant indicated to Ridley the glass of whisky on the coffee table, and a cigarette that had burned down all the way to the filter in the ashtray – the ash long and unbroken.

Grant put his finger to his lips.

Ridley nodded approvingly.

They both took out their weapons. It was time to prepare for the worst.

CHAPTER EIGHTEEN

Outside, the hillside was swept by a stiff wind breaking across the heather and the long wispy grass. It sounded like a meditative track from a 'Relaxing Sounds' playlist. The loch's waters gently lapped nearby, unseen, somewhere out in the gathering gloom. A tranquil contrast to the occasional, ominous whistle of the wind.

On the hillside overlooking Faraday's cottage, tufts of tall grass and patches of heather suddenly stirred. A camouflage-clad figure emerged, signalling towards the cottage. Soon several more sections of grass and heather rose, revealing armed men, each with a submachine gun, their faces steely with determination. They had their orders, and they would carry them out unwaveringly.

Back in Faraday's cottage, Grant remained oblivious to the impending threat creeping down the hillside. With Ridley having cleared the other rooms, Grant's focus narrowed to the kitchen – the last refuge where Faraday might hide.

Spotting a prone figure on the floor – unmistakably Faraday – Grant muttered a curse, 'Shit...Ridley, kitchen!'

Grant dashed towards Faraday, who lay motionless on his back.

Ridley ran in after him. 'Is he dead?'

Kneeling beside Faraday, Grant assessed the situation. 'I don't know – he's not breathing...' Before he could administer CPR or do anything else, a loud click from Ridley's direction froze him. He didn't even have to turn around to know what was happening. Grant shut his eyes and cursed himself for breaking Winston's cardinal rule: *the lesson isn't trust no one, Grant. The lesson is trust me...*

Ridley's tone darkened as he levelled his gun. 'I can't let you do that, Grant,' he said.

Grant turned slowly to face him, hands raised. 'What the hell are you doing, Ridley?' he asked.

'My job,' Ridley replied tersely.

Ridley went on, 'If you knew what I knew, you'd be doing exactly the same. I was going to let you disappear. I tried to convince them, but they wouldn't let me. I want you to know that. I'm not callous. But it could just as easily be me with the gun in my face right now.'

'At least tell me why,' Grant said.

Ridley was impressed by Grant's composure. It clearly wasn't the first time he'd had a gun pointed at him. 'Why? How the hell should I know? All I know is that this op is my fast-track out of Section 7 in favour of a cushy little number at a nice embassy. Somewhere warm and sunny would be nice. I'll need to work that out with John Wark, but for now, I'll be happy just to no longer have madmen chasing after me with Section 7.'

Grant snorted with contempt. 'You were never cut out for field work. Always took the easy option.'

Ridley moved swiftly to one side, keeping a distance away from Grant, never underestimating his resourcefulness. But in focussing all his attention on Grant, Ridley didn't notice Faraday's hand moving towards a holster on his ankle.

Ridley took aim at Grant's chest, ready to fire. 'It's nothing per–'

But before he could fire, he caught a flash of black somewhere in his peripheral vision near Faraday, then the glint of a blade as it slashed across his achilles. Ridley screamed from a searing agony the likes of which he hadn't thought possible. For a moment, he thought his entire foot had been severed from his leg.

He dropped his gun, and grabbed at his ankle which was pouring blood like a geyser, spraying across the linoleum floor. He whipped around towards Faraday, who was now standing, clutching a bloody hunting knife.

Before Ridley could react further, Faraday slammed the knife into Ridley's chest. He held it in, pulling Ridley in close. He had a Cockney accent, the sort of voice that should have been yelling out the price of fish down a market on a weekday morning. 'Should have checked vitals, sunshine. Appearances can be deceptive. And details can get you killed.'

Faraday retracted the knife, then let Ridley fall back. He was dead before he hit the floor.

Grant pulled his gun and pointed it at Faraday, who didn't seem remotely troubled.

Faraday rummaged through Ridley's pockets, found nothing, then he pulled out a flesh-coloured earbud from Ridley's left ear.

'You see him put that in?' asked Faraday.

'No, I...' Grant was reeling. 'It must have been when we got out the car.'

Faraday held the bud up to his ear, then he motioned for Grant to get down. 'They're coming. We have to move. Now.'

'What the hell is going on?' Grant asked.

Faraday marched from drawer to cupboard, arming himself with stashed weapons. 'I've got motion-sensor cameras hanging in the tree at the end of the garden. A couple of guys tripped it an hour ago.'

'You've been lying on the ground playing dead all that time?' Grant asked.

Faraday slid a short knife into a holster on his ankle. Then he loaded a Heckler & Koch submachine gun he took out of a cupboard next to the cooker.

As kitchens went, it wasn't exactly childproof.

Faraday said, 'Playing dead seemed like the best option at the time...' He ran to the living room to turn off the TV, then he dashed back. He turned off the last of the lights, then motioned for Grant to stay low.

Grant asked, 'How did you know Ridley was going to–'

'I didn't. I've just assumed that every single person who's driven along this road in the past eleven years has been coming to kill me. Now it's going to take a minor miracle for either one of us to get out this place alive.'

'We were supposed to be here to extract you and take you to a safe house. Someone's been–'

Faraday nodded like it was old news. 'Killing Albions. Yeah, I get it Grant.'

'You know my name?'

'What I know and what you don't would take up cover to cover of *War and Peace*. Don't worry about how I know what I know. Olivia Christie's played you like a pound-shop ukulele, son. You weren't brought here to save me. You were brought here to be executed. Like me.'

Grant hesitated. He couldn't get his options clear in his head. For someone who prided himself on preparing for anything, nothing could have prepared him for this.

As for Christie setting him up, Grant refused to believe it.

Seeking to clarify things, Faraday said, 'I'm sorry, do you want to spend a few minutes mourning the guy who was about to put a bullet in your head? Because there's a whole squad of his sort,' he gestured at Ridley, 'coming down the hillside. You can take your chances with me or them. Your choice.'

Grant wiped his face with his hand, trying to mentally reset. He leaned down to get a look out the kitchen window facing the back garden. The men outside were moving quietly, but there was no question that they were moving in fast.

Grant shook his head. 'Looks like I'm stuck with you either way. It's too late to run.'

Faraday reached under the kitchen table and pulled out a double-barrel shotgun. He told Grant, 'All I really wanted was a quiet life.' He cocked the shotgun, preparing to fire. 'Looks like that ship has sailed.'

CHAPTER NINETEEN

GRANT AND FARADAY crouched below the worktop, communicating only in hand signals and gestures now. Slowly but surely, they could feel the team outside closing in somewhere out in the darkness. Two cars were approaching from either side of the cottage, their headlights off, but it was impossible not to hear them in the peaceful surroundings. The team didn't appear to be making any secret that they were there. Grant and Faraday braced themselves as car doors were shut. Footsteps on the gravel approached, with murmured whispers and the shuffling of feet as the team hurried to get into position.

As the more senior and experienced of the two, and knowing the property, Faraday took the lead, pointing at the long kitchen table then the back door.

Grant nodded affirmatively, then quickly dragged the table over to the door. With Faraday's help, he turned it longways, barricading the door.

Faraday then pulled the blinds down on the windows. He mouthed to Grant, 'Stay out the centre of the room.'

Grant nodded again. It was a pointer that he didn't need,

knowing from experience and training that stray bullets were much more likely to take you out in the middle of an open space.

With the blinds closed and the lights turned off, the two men were left in almost complete darkness. The sounds of the team advancing and preparing to attack heightened their senses.

Grant held his gun at the ready, taking some steadying breaths. There was a good chance that he wasn't going to get out of there on anything but a coroner's stretcher.

Then everything was silent.

Grant looked left. Then right.

Faraday was much less twitchy. Like a snake, he stayed perfectly still, waiting for movement in his peripheral vision to guide him.

Then a shadow moved in the living room.

In a quick, flawless motion, Faraday blasted his shotgun in the shadow's direction, sending the first of the siege team catapulting backwards.

The sound of the blast set off a wave of fire all around the kitchen. All the windows were shot out in a matter of seconds, leaving the blinds swaying from the impact of the bullets. It was such an onslaught, Grant and Faraday had no option but to take temporary cover. Standing up to return fire would have been suicide.

Plaster and glass rained down on the men, while bullets whizzed right over their heads.

The men knew the team were trying to batter them into submission with pure brute force of fire. A sign that the lead man on the ground wasn't confident in his men's abilities.

As Grant and Faraday huddled close to one another on the

kitchen floor, a brief look between them seemed to communicate everything necessary.

The gunfire relented for a moment, but the team weren't hanging around outside. A creak on the decking alerted Grant to someone behind the window. Grant couldn't make anything out through the bullet holes in the blind. Still, he let off multiple shots, then saw two bodies falling over each other – both men letting out groans on the way down.

With the loss of two of their own, the team leader ordered a return to brute force. Someone rammed the back door, sending the kitchen table flying backwards. With the door off its hinges, there was now a clear doorway out into the night. The team poured in, guns blazing. But Grant and Faraday had seen it coming, and had already taken up a defensive position behind the table, and right under the noses of the advancing operatives.

Faraday stood up and blasted the first man in, blowing him right out the doorway he'd just come through.

Grant backed Faraday up by taking out the two men close behind the first.

A bright spotlight came on outside, lighting up the kitchen. Grant and Faraday recoiled from the startling brightness, after hiding in the dark.

The team outside now had a perfect view of their movements in the kitchen.

Faraday was quickest to see the danger. During a brief respite from gunfire, he whispered, 'Move move move…'

The safest place to be was on either side of the door, taking occasional peeks out to fire. It was risky, but it was the only way to stop anyone else advancing.

More charged through from the living room, leaving Grant and Faraday surrounded.

Grant dealt with the operatives coming from the living

room, while Faraday dealt with the ones outside, evidently gleeful at their beating the odds of an unfair fight so far.

Grant was sure he actually heard Faraday laughing at one point while guns were going off all around.

As Faraday kept shooting, Grant saw the blinds twitch across the room. Grant dashed over – his figure illuminated by the spotlight for a moment – while Faraday covered him. Grant pulled the blind back, revealing in the harshness of the spotlight, an operative pointing his weapon straight at Faraday's back. Grant fired just in time, sending the man to his knees, then Grant fired three more times, taking out a man with each bullet.

Faraday let off more shotgun blasts, managing to take out the spotlight with his final bullet.

While Faraday reloaded, Grant yelled, 'How many have they got out there?'

'Not as many as they started with,' Faraday yelled back, pumping the shotgun one-handed.

Then silence again.

The team leader had pulled his remaining operatives out of the back garden.

Grant held his hands out as if to say, *is that it over?*

Faraday held a finger up to indicate *one moment*. Then he put the finger to his lips for silence.

With the faintest sound underneath the floorboards, Faraday pointed at the floor with urgency.

Grant hadn't noticed it yet, but there was a pull-up door in the floor leading to a basement. He scuttled across the room, taking aim at the door.

Faraday did the same at the opposite side.

Despite the chill in the air, Grant was sweating.

Faraday stared at the door with a ferocious intensity.

The room turned silent again. Not so much as a tap from under the floorboards.

Grant nearly retracted his weapon, when the pull-up door flew open, and one man stood up, clutching a shotgun. Faraday was first to react.

He blasted the man backwards, pinning him back against the door opening. As the other men behind him retreated out of the basement, Grant followed the sound of the men scrambling out. He threw the blinds aside, then fired at the last of the team, who was on his hands and knees, trying to escape from the basement window that led to the garden.

The mistake Grant made was thinking it was over.

He whipped around expecting to see a smiling Faraday pleased with his work. Instead, he saw a man standing at the open window opposite, his submachine gun pointing at Grant's chest.

Faraday was already on it, but he could only get off a round after the man at the window had fired.

The man got off one bullet before Faraday's shotgun thundered twice, putting him down.

Grant twisted and writhed in agony as he felt the bullet go into his stomach, then he collapsed to the floor.

Faraday ran over to him and hauled Grant to his feet. 'Come on,' wheezed Faraday. 'We've got to get out of here…' Then he saw Grant's eyes widen at something beyond the kitchen. Outside.

The team leader: the last man.

With both hands around Grant, Faraday couldn't get a shot away in time.

Through gritted teeth, Grant managed to raise his gun somehow, firing two bullets at the last man. Grant kept pulling the trigger after his clip had emptied.

Faraday huffed in relief.

'You okay?' asked Grant.

Faraday grinned. 'You're the one who's been shot.'

He led them out to the back garden. A quick assessment of the scene told him that they were in the clear.

Against all the odds, the pair of them were getting out of there.

'You have somewhere we can go?' Grant asked.

'Not really.' Faraday hauled Grant down the driveway towards the Range Rover he and Ridley had arrived in.

On the way past the dead body of the lead man, Grant tapped Faraday on the shoulder and told him to stop.

'What is it?' Faraday asked.

Grant crouched down to feel the man's pockets. Then he reached in and took out the man's mobile phone, along with his radio earpiece. Grant handed it to Faraday, who listened to the radio on the move.

After listening for a few seconds, Grant asked, 'Anything?'

Faraday chucked the earpiece having heard everything he needed to hear. 'They're all down anyway. We got the last man. Control room sounds like chaos.'

'Yeah, I'll bet,' Grant replied.

Faraday shoved Grant into the passenger seat, then asked, 'You ever gone off map before?'

Grant held a hand at his stomach wound, wincing. 'Briefly,' he said.

Faraday started the engine, then reversed faster than most people drive going forwards.

Grant asked, 'What about you? You ever gone off map before?'

Faraday looked at him and smiled. 'Keep a hand on that wound. We've got a bit of a drive ahead.'

CHAPTER TWENTY

FOREIGN SECRETARY JOHN WARK couldn't have looked more at home in the Pugin Room Members' dining and lounge room, deep in the Houses of Parliament. Originally a peers' committee room, it had undergone extensive – and tax-payer funded – renovations. It bore all the hallmarks of a traditional gentlemen's club, an oasis of grandeur and ostentatious luxury. The walls were decked in Gothic tapestry wallpaper, with Victorian-style furniture, and numerous gilt brass and crystal chandeliers.

This was what John Wark had been destined for since childhood. Packed off to boarding school before he could ride a bike, then private school at all the places you would expect to find a future Foreign Secretary. His ascendancy through the ranks of the British political elite couldn't have been any more inevitable.

He was surrounded by four of his closest allies, drinking whiskies and nibbling at canapés in preparation for a late dinner in the Churchill Grill Room down the corridor.

Wark's aide approached nervously, holding a mobile phone

tight against his chest. 'Sir, I apologise for interrupting. I've got the Prime Minister on the line.'

That prompted a few raised eyebrows around the table.

Wark scoffed. 'I'll call him back, Edward.'

The aide thought about leaving, then had second thoughts. 'It's just...he was calling to remind you that he's pushed back dinner twice now in order to squeeze you in.'

Wark muttered under his breath, 'Squeeze me in...What does it matter if his dinner's been pushed back twice. He's a fifty-year-old widower. Who's he going to have dinner with? The cleaning staff?'

Even by Wark's standards it was a low blow, and he seemed to realise it. He wiped the smile from his face. 'Tell him I'll be there soon.'

The aide scuttled off, waiting until he was somewhere quieter before delivering the news.

Wark smirked at the others. 'Bloody PM...I swear there's a car showroom somewhere missing a manager.'

The others laughed.

'Maybe not long if the polls continue on their current trajectory,' said one.

'I think it's time for a change, John. I know I'm not the only one who thinks so.'

Wark did his best impression of modesty – a feeling that he had never felt once, genuinely, in his life. He groaned as he saw his aide returning once more with the phone. 'Oh Edward, piss off,' Wark complained.

Edward held his ground. 'I'm sorry, sir...' He didn't know how to say it. He didn't even really know what it meant. 'It's Albion. That's all she told me to say.'

Wark's smile vanished. He snatched the phone from Edward, then took it over to the large French windows that led out to a patio area. There were two backbenchers smoking cigars.

Wark covered the phone mouthpiece, then told the backbenchers, 'Sorry, gents, I need to take this.'

Without a flicker of complaint, the men ditched their cigars and went inside.

Once he was alone, Wark said, 'Yeah?'

The voice at the other end was Olivia Christie's. 'The Albions got away,' she said.

Wark leaned over the balcony. '*Both* of them?' Wark spat, 'I knew that weasel Ridley wouldn't be up to it–'

Christie explained, 'John, Ridley's dead. They're all dead.'

Wark didn't know what to do with himself. 'The whole team? How is that possible?'

'We're still assessing.'

'*Assessing?*' He struggled to keep his voice down. 'You'll be assessing the current job market for menopausal bureaucrats next week if you don't take control of this.'

'It's being handled, John.'

Wark hung up. He needed a moment to collect his thoughts. Then he let out a long exhalation. He dialled a number on his phone. The moment they picked up, Wark said, 'That thing you promised wouldn't happen has just happened. It's time for plan B.'

CHAPTER TWENTY-ONE

OLIVIA CHRISTIE HAD CALLED in the most experienced staff with the highest clearance from across the European Task floor, and assembled them in the Crisis Suite of the third floor. They had a full grid and comms system in place. Everything was state-of-the-art. Her team was highly motivated, working on a complex arrangement of bonus structures on top of their regular salaries – which were already significant.

It was a team of the smartest, quickest minds in MI6, all highly invested in achieving whatever result Christie desired.

Having the Director herself leading a task was unusual in itself. The silence surrounding the mystery of Leo Winston's absence only adding fuel to a rumour mill that had been in overdrive since earlier that evening.

Upon Christie's arrival in the room, every analyst straightened in their chairs, ready to get to work. All they knew was that a mission had been called and it was short notice.

'Okay, people,' Christie announced. 'This is a Priority Two situation. Get me faces on the board, please...'

The video wall at the front of the room switched to

photographs of Duncan Grant on one side and Robert Faraday on the other. Two faces that no one in the room other than Christie knew.

'This one's going to be a little different,' she explained. 'These two are ours. Grant is still active. Faraday is retired: note, that photo is twenty years old. We're working on an update.' She pointed to the relevant part of the screen for satellite images.

The team was used to dealing with congested suburban areas. Large, major cities, tracking people through complex transport networks and roads. What they were looking at was almost unique. A map almost entirely green and brown. At the centre was a long thin strip of black, showing the water of Loch Naver. Halfway along it on the north bank was a pulsing red dot.

Christie pointed at it. 'This is our last-known location. Two ways in, two ways out. There's not a camera for a hundred miles, so don't bother looking. Our targets will no doubt believe this to be something in their favour. Grant will have had access to a black agency Range Rover. The registration is on the screen. Familiarise yourself with it, because you're going to be saying it and typing it for however many hours it takes for us to find it. Grant's good. Faraday is even better. So they'll know they can make a move in this car, but only for so long.'

An analyst, convinced that he had done a bang-up job, said, 'I've got us up on every camera within a hundred miles. It will take a bit of time, but eventually they'll need to hit an A road and we'll snare them.'

Christie paced in front of the video wall, arms folded, unimpressed. 'That's great,' she said, masking her disappointment. 'Except, Grant and Faraday have already thought of that. No chance they'll run that Range Rover into proximity of road cameras. What we need is to track every vehicle tied to within twenty miles of that site, so we need to access DCLA.' She pointed to the coordinates of Faraday's cottage. 'That's ground zero. I want a list of those vehicles circulated and on the network within fifteen minutes. One by one, we flag anything that moves outside of a fifty-mile radius of ground zero. We clear each and every vehicle until we're certain it's not Grant or Faraday. I don't care if it's something that hasn't moved in three years, or if it's a bloody tractor. You don't wipe it from your list until you're certain. They don't have much in the way of transportation options, and they can't hide in the countryside like *The Thirty-Nine* bloody *Steps*. It's Sutherland. Picture Iceland, but with far fewer tourists.' She gestured with her arms to rouse everyone. 'Everyone on this, now! Let's go...'

She leaned over to a man named Connolly, the most senior technician and analyst in the room.

'I need an asset up and on his feet,' Christie told him. 'The objective here isn't capture. I need something more definitive.'

Connolly was slow to react. It was early in an operation to be calling in an asset. 'Yes, ma'am.'

Christie watched the room spring into action, then she stared at Grant's picture on the wall. It was important to remain professional in such a situation, but she couldn't help herself thinking, *'I'm sorry, Duncan.'*

CHAPTER TWENTY-TWO

Grant was struggling to maintain pressure on his bullet wound. Blood was continuing to seep through the tiny gaps between his fingers. Faraday had passed him a blanket from the back seat, but Grant found that soft material didn't plug the wound tightly enough.

'Robert,' Grant groaned, 'I need help. I'm not going to make it long like this.'

Faraday kept his eyes on the road ahead. He was travelling well beyond what anyone would call a safe speed for such a narrow and twisting road. 'I know, Duncan, but I don't have anywhere to take you yet. I need you to hold on. The nearest place you'll get help is Inverness or Ullapool. And I can't take you to a hospital at either of those places.'

'Just go, man. I'll take my chances.'

'Duncan, they'll have a black bag over your head or another bullet in you before you've been stitched up. The first priority is getting all eyes off us, so I can take you somewhere that's safe.'

'Where?' asked Grant.

Faraday paused, knowing the effect it would have on Grant's state of mind. 'Far away...'

Grant shut his eyes and turned his head up in dismay.

Faraday went on, 'But once we get there, I can get us fixed up with clean slates.'

In desperation, Grant said, 'We need to just ditch this car and take a local's. It's getting late. It won't be hard to find one at the next property we see.'

Faraday peered into the rear-view mirror, checking for cars following with their headlights off. But there was nothing. 'That's exactly what they're counting on,' he said. 'They'll have eyes up on every car within twenty miles of here by now. And as soon as one of them steps outside a radius of fifty miles – maybe less – they'll have an entire team descending on it.'

Grant moaned as he adjusted his position slightly, opening the stomach wound a little which brought a tidal wave of pain through his whole body. 'What do you suggest then?'

'A contingency,' Faraday said. 'One I thought I would never need.'

A few miles outside of Lairg, a tiny village at the southern bank of Loch Shin, Faraday pulled onto a dirt track leading up to a farm on a hillside overlooking the loch. There was one light on in the cottage at the end of the track.

Faraday had to leave Grant in the Range Rover while he spoke with the man at the front door. Before Faraday left, the men shook hands, then the man grabbed his coat and walked quickly over to his own car. A traditional green 1996 Land Rover Defender. It had seen better days, but it could still get up a twenty per cent gradient without breaking a sweat.

Faraday went back to Grant and told him, 'Come on, we're swapping.'

Grant hobbled out with Faraday's help.

Then the man appeared from his garage, holding a replacement registration plate. Once Faraday had helped Grant into the passenger seat of the old Land Rover, he changed the plate.

Faraday let the man drive off in the MI6 Range Rover first.

'What the hell is going on?' asked Grant.

'Tommy there is heading for John O'Groats.'

'John O'Groats? It must be a hundred miles from here.'

Faraday set off again, turning left out of the driveway and continuing south. 'Eighty-eight, actually.'

'Why is he going there?'

'To cash out the favour I paid him for a long time ago.'

Grant was in too much pain to ask anything further.

CHAPTER TWENTY-THREE

Back in the MI6 Crisis Suite an hour later, Christie was in a huddle with two analysts who were showing her car registrations they thought worth tracking. Then a call came up from a desk along with a raised hand.

'Ma'am! I think I've got something.'

Christie went straight over. 'What is it?'

The analyst went through the data on his screen. 'Nineteen ninety-six Land Rover Defender. Registered to a Thomas Bonnar. Address listed is somewhere called Lairg...' He zoomed in on the map on his screen which showed the route travelled so far. 'Based on where we've clocked the car on the A9 just south of Brora, it looks like it's going up to Wick. Maybe John O'Groats.'

Christie paused, assessing the map. She said to herself, 'The timing would fit. Lairg's a good place to dump a car before you reach cameras on the A9. And heading north is a smart move. All the major airports and roads are south. Why not head north instead...unexpected. High-risk. Smart move.'

The analyst went on, 'There's also Thurso. Could be trying for a morning ferry.'

'Where does the ferry go to?'

'Orkney.'

Christie tapped on the screen on the small island just north of John O'Groats. 'They're going for Kirkwall Airport on Orkney.'

'If they do that, then they could follow on to Shetland–'

Christie could see it now. 'And then Bergen in Norway. There are flights twice a week to Norway and then we're screwed. Get me armed resources on that car.'

The analyst did a double-take. 'That might be a challenge at this time of night, ma'am, in that location.'

Christie snapped, 'Make it happen!' When she whipped around and faced the glass entrance to the suite, she saw Leo Winston standing there, having been scanned by security in the blackout room outside – a clearing space for staff to enter and exit the Crisis Suite, without giving a view into the suite from the corridor outside.

Christie met him at the door. 'Leo, what the hell are you doing here?'

'My job,' he said. 'Trying to stop someone from killing my man out there.'

He was wearing a polo neck, which obscured the large bandage covering the abrasion wound around his neck. He looked frail and gaunt, and despite his typically strong frame, there was something about the way he was carrying himself that made him look weak.

Christie said, 'You're not in full possession of the facts, Leo.'

'Oh, really? Because I thought you were running the Crisis Suite to take out Grant and Faraday.'

'It's time to wrap up Albion, Leo. It was a mistake. I should never have brought it back.'

Albion was the last thing on Winston's mind. 'You're going to kill him. Aren't you?'

Used to dealing in euphemisms, it finally felt freeing to for once use plain language. 'There's no other choice.'

'But our own guy?'

Christie led him away to a quiet corner. 'The other people in this room haven't had to swallow a fraction of what we have in our careers. We love our country, Leo. That's why we do this job. We want to protect people. Grant's gone off the rails once too often. He jeopardised billions when he killed Henry Marlow before securing the password for the stolen funds. He had no idea Randall would be able to break the code. It was a personal vendetta.'

It was Winston's turn to lose his temper now, struggling to keep his voice down. 'Then we bring him in! Debrief. Tie off his profile, then send him home.'

Christie shook her head. 'Not an Albion. Not someone who's demonstrated consistent pattens of rogue behaviour. It's escalating, Winston, can't you see that? Where does it end? You *knew* this was the contingency if things went south with an Albion, so don't pretend your eyes weren't open. I asked you to bring Grant in, and instead you decided to hit the booze again and...'

Winston turned away in disgust.

Christie tutted. 'Leo,' she said softly, 'I've got a dozen guys lying dead in a cottage in the middle of nowhere up there. We have no idea what Grant and Faraday's intentions are now. But the facts that we do have are that they have murdered MI6 extraction personnel, and I don't know why.'

Winston stared deep into her eyes, assessing her the way he

used to assess a source. 'Look at me and tell me that team wasn't sent there to kill Grant.'

Without hesitation, Christie replied confidently, 'The team wasn't sent there to kill Grant. It was an extraction team that Grant was supposed to be a part of. I was the one who briefed him and Ridley for god's sake.'

'Ridley's dead too?' asked Winston.

'They're all dead, Leo! So now we have to make the difficult decisions. Together. But I need you on this. I can't run these grids like you.'

Winston looked over to the video wall, getting himself up to speed with what they were doing. 'Okay,' he said. 'Give me ten minutes to get myself together.'

Christie nodded.

The moment he was out of the blackout room, Winston ran to the stairs as best he could, in too much of a hurry to wait for a lift. When he got to the floor below, he dashed along a corridor that was lined with offices. At the very end was a pale light, and the faint sound of classical music.

Träumerei composed by Robert Schumann.

It was a pianist playing a mournful but beautiful melody. Not that Winston was focussing on such things right now.

Randall looked up from his work, surrounded by excess office furniture. He was pleasantly surprised to see Winston. 'Leo! I was wondering where you'd got to.' Without realising Winston's sense of urgency, Randall looked back down at his work. 'If there's a better pianist than Vladimir Horowitz, then I've never heard them. Listen to the simplicity of that phrasing. So delicate yet authoritative. With Horowitz, there's none of that grandstanding you see from the young pianists these days. Pulling faces as if they're about to weep. So phony. You know, they say that composing this is what made Schumann mad. He should have just come to work in this place instead.' Randall snorted a laugh, then looked up.

The way Winston failed to respond in kind, told him something was amiss.

Randall asked, 'What's going on?'

Winston said, 'Randall, I need someone I can trust.'

Randall dropped his pen. 'Of course.'

'It's Duncan. He needs our help.'

CHAPTER TWENTY-FOUR

Tommy Bonnar was driving up the north-east coast feeling pretty good about life. He'd had a windfall from the unlikeliest of sources, and all for the strangest of requests: to drive to John O'Groats, stay there for six hours, and then drive back.

Not that Robert Faraday expected Bonnar to make it that far – although Faraday had neglected to mention that part of his plan.

A builder by trade his entire life, jobs were few and far between when they did come in that neck of the woods. So to be compensated to the tune of ten thousand pounds for a minor inconvenience and the possibility of not seeing his car again, seemed a fair deal to Tommy.

It was a quiet road at the best of times, even as the main road to a village famous for being the most distant point on the British mainland from Land's End all the way down in Cornwall. Often mistaken as the most northerly point on the British mainland, it had in fact garnered its reputation thanks to a savvy photography company, who installed what would become a famous signpost known as 'Journey's End', and noted the distance to, among other places, Land's End, New York, and Shetland. Installed on private land, the company charged a few for tourists to have their picture taken next to it. Little did they know that technically the most northerly point on the British mainland was some thirty miles west at Dunnet Head.

The A9 ran next to the North Sea for long stretches, and Bonnar had experienced the frightening gales that whipped off from the east. The wind had been steadily picking up since he'd left, and there had barely been another vehicle on the road since the last village at Brora.

So when he saw four sets of headlights one behind the other and speeding towards him from behind, Bonnar looked in his rear-view mirror in curiosity.

That quickly gave way to fear and panic, though, when all four vehicles lit up their blue flashing lights and sirens.

Bonnar, who had been puttering along in his Land Rover, was soon overtaken by two of the police cars, with the other two staying at the back to box him in.

Bonnar slowed to a stop, muttering to himself in his thick Sutherland accent, 'Whit the fuck...Jesus, Robert, whit the hell did ye dae?'

Armed officers charged at the car in well-rehearsed formation, weapons pulled.

Shaking like a leaf, Bonnar put his hands on the steering wheel as instructed, then he was met with a sudden burst of wind off the sea as an officer in full combat gear threw his door open, and ripped Bonnar out of his seat. He tossed Bonnar onto the road, face-first, and patted him down.

'Where are the others?' the officer demanded.

Helpless and terrified, Bonnar pleaded, 'Whit others? I've no got anybody else wae me!'

The other officers searched the rest of the car, opening the boot, lifting up the spare tyre in the back. The officer at the back shook his head to the point man crouched over Bonnar to say 'no.'

Another turned away and got his on his radio back to control in Inverness, where they had just raced from, scrambled into action after a series of phone calls with the highest ranking police officers in Scotland and the Home Office.

IN THE CRISIS SUITE, news petered through from the road.

'Shit,' Christie cursed, turning away from the video wall, which showed live body cam footage from an officer with Bonnar.

The air filled with further profanity as Bonnar was bundled off for interrogation.

'Ah've no done nothin'...' he complained.

Standing next to Christie, Winston said, 'He played you.'

'You mean us,' said Christie. 'And now where have they gone when we've been looking the other way?'

Winston let out a weary sigh. 'I don't know, Olivia. We'll start over. Hopefully we can get something out of the driver.'

Christie took out her phone. 'I need to make a call.'

Once she was gone, Winston hid a smile behind his hand. 'Good lad, Duncan...Whatever you did up there, good lad.'

CHAPTER TWENTY-FIVE

The journey south had been mostly a blur to Grant, of darkness, occasional flickers of light from passing cars, and a newfound respect for the suspension in modern cars. The Land Rover had proven a valuable – yet highly uncomfortable – asset. Grant's seat was only marginally better than sitting on a plastic stool.

Once they got over Dornoch Firth bridge, Grant could feel the pain becoming impossible to deal with. Having pulled over twice to assess the wound, Faraday had declared Grant's chances of bleeding out as 'in the low thirties as a percentage.'

It had been intended to instil calm in Grant, but had actually had the opposite effect.

'Will you just tell me where we're going?' Grant begged. 'If I know how far it is–'

Faraday interrupted, 'You'll go out of your mind. What good would it do? Would it be helpful if I said it'll be another fifty miles? Or what about a hundred?' Faraday indicated with a gesture near his temple. 'You've got to just flick that little switch in your head that tells you to deal with the pain. Settle in it. Exist with it. If I give you a timeframe, it will be you telling your brain to pump a tsunami of cortisol through your body. And you don't need that right now. Your body's got enough to deal with.'

Grant's hopes were lifted by the sight of Kessock Bridge which led into Inverness. The sheer granite wall that ran next to the left side of the road tapered off on the approach to the bridge. Then the view suddenly opened up to the vast expanse of the Moray Firth. After so much time without road lights, the ones on the bridge appeared much brighter than they actually were. Coming from the miles of empty space in Sutherland, little Inverness appeared as sprawling and industrial as Glasgow. Grant had never been so happy to see articulated lorries on the road. It felt like some kind of return to civilisation.

And with it, the promise of healthcare.

'Hold on,' said Faraday, coming off the motorway for the Raigmore Interchange.

Grant got his hopes up that their journey was nearly at an end.

But Faraday had a different idea.

He drove into the twenty-four-hour Tesco Extra, then told Grant, 'Two seconds.'

Grant replied, 'No one has ever used that phrase and only taken two seconds. Try again.'

Faraday relented. 'Five, six minutes.'

He parked in a dark corner of the car park, then left Grant alone for what felt like an eternity. Faraday returned with what was surely up there with the strangest baskets to ever grace a self-checkout.

Grant had curled up in his seat, in desperate search for

more warmth. His internal temperature had plummeted, as his bodily resources were ploughed into keeping him alive.

Faraday emptied the plastic bag one item at a time, making the preparations.

Grant was only vaguely aware of what was going on. Faraday appeared to have bought items at random.

There were some bandages and co-codamol to start.

Grant mentioned, 'You do know I haven't just got a wee headache, right?'

'Patience,' Faraday told him. He also had two bottles of water, two bags of frozen peas, some kids' party cups, and some coffee filters. 'You need more codeine than your body can safely process with all the paracetamol they load these pills up with. That's why you need to extract the good stuff, and get rid of the stuff that will make you OD.'

Faraday went about pouring water into one of the party cups that was decorated with balloons on the side. Then he attached a coffee filter over another empty cup, then set about mashing up a dozen of the pills.

Taken straight out of the foil packets, it would have been a dangerous load for a liver to deal with. Hence Faraday's plan. Otherwise known as a Cold Water Extraction.

Faraday mashed the pills into a powder using a AAA battery from the glove compartment – the perfect size, weight, and density to grind it down as small as possible. Which was crucial to the process. Without it, larger granules meant a higher chance of leaving dangerous levels of paracetamol in the mixture.

Once the powder was mixed in the water, having been filtered through into the cup, Faraday took the two bags of frozen peas and held them tight against the sides of the cup. 'Cooling the mixture helps with the filtration process,' he explained, then realised Grant's mind was elsewhere. 'All you need to know is that this will take the edge off. And then some. Make you dream sweet dreams until we get to my friend's place to patch you up.'

That there was actually a concrete plan came as a revelation to Grant, though he found it impossible to show it.

Once the mixture in the cup had cooled for five minutes, Faraday handed it to Grant. He held onto the cup himself, feeding it to Grant as if he was a small child. He couldn't risk Grant dropping it, and having to start the process all over again.

'Drink it up,' said Faraday, tilting the cup to Grant's mouth. 'Get it all down you, son.'

Grant recoiled from the strong pasty taste, then a few seconds later he started to feel relief.

Faraday smiled, 'Hits you quick, doesn't it. That's a heck of a Saturday night for most people that.'

They were soon back on the road.

Now that the pain had died down, Grant felt like talking more.

He asked, 'So how does a cockney like you end up living somewhere like Sutherland?'

'I like quiet places,' said Faraday. 'It doesn't get much quieter than Sutherland. For a lot of people, driving twenty miles if you need a loaf of bread is a turn off. For me, that's what I wanted when I got out.'

'You know you're one of the lucky ones.'

'Is that what it was? Luck? Was it luck that got us out that cottage tonight, and all?'

'Point taken,' replied Grant.

'So Olivia Christie brought back Albion?'

'I don't think it was a popular choice, but she had the Foreign Sec over a barrel.'

'What did she have on him? Love child? Affair? Wark seems the sort, the sleazy bastard.'

'It was work. I found evidence that he'd been involved in the assassination of Kadir Rashid. He was a journalist who–'

'I know about Rashid, Duncan. It's a long walk to a newsagent around Loch Naver. That doesn't mean I don't have the internet.'

'What no one reported about Rashid's assassination is that the job was at first farmed out to an Albion operative.'

'Who?'

'Henry Marlow?'

'Marlow? Jesus wept. He was a psycho back then, I'm sure he's still a psycho.'

'Not so much.'

Faraday paused. 'Dead?'

'I should say so. I was the one who killed him.'

Faraday waited for an explanation.

Grant explained, 'He went rogue on the Rashid job. Disappeared. It upset the wrong people. Marlow went totally sideways after that. Started a proxy war against the agency, teaming up with war lords like Charles Joseph. He didn't want money or power in the end. He just wanted to burn the whole world down.'

Faraday said, 'That explains why they wanted Marlow dead. Why did you do it?'

'Because he killed someone close to me.' Grant hesitated to use the word. 'Someone I loved. I couldn't let him walk away from it.'

As the lights of cars on the other side of the A9 illuminated Faraday, Grant had a little more time to take him in. His face was almost entirely bereft of fat. Everything was in sharp lines. His cheeks. His jaw. His nose. A severe look.

Like a mountainside carved and shaped by millennia of rainfall.

'So it was about honour, was it?' asked Faraday.

'Something like that,' Grant replied, but his mind was elsewhere. 'Did it make you happy, living out there on your own?'

'Solitude's the only thing that makes me happy. What about you?'

'Same.'

'And what's your plan?'

'What do you mean?'

'To get out. You need a plan. Or do you think you're going to do this for the rest of your life? Albions don't age well, Duncan. It's like that old adage about "show me an obese ninety-year-old".'

'There were a few Albions who made it into retirement.'

'They didn't last, either. It always catches up to them in the end.'

'So you know about the others?'

'Of course I do. I might have been far away, but word has a habit of reaching the people it needs to.'

'Who do you think would want something like that to happen? To kill former Albions?'

Faraday pursed his lips. 'I don't know.'

It was true he had been out the game for a while. He'd also been on his own for too long. Because Grant immediately spotted his lie.

Eager to change the subject, Faraday said, 'When you realise that everything you risked your life for was a waste of time, the idea of doing nothing has great appeal. What looks like doing nothing, is simply staying alive. It's underrated, staying alive. Believe me. And if you don't, just ask the dead.'

Grant found it hard to argue with that one

Faraday continued, 'You remind me of the ronin.'

'I don't know what that is.'

'They were a warrior class of samurai in feudal Japan. They dedicated their lives to protecting their masters. In that world, there was nothing as shameful as a samurai whose master was allowed to be killed. If that ever happened, the samurai were forced to wander the earth as bandits. Hired help. But they weren't called samurai anymore once their masters were slain. They were called ronin. There was a famous story about forty-seven ronin. Their master was betrayed and killed. These samurai – ronin – they became different people, invented new identities, lived different lives. They even faked madness. For three years this went on. Plotting their revenge. Until finally they found the castle of the man who had killed their master. They took their revenge, killing him. Then, once it was done, all forty-seven of them committed seppuku outside the castle. A ritualistic slitting of their stomachs.'

Grant didn't say anything.

Faraday looked at him for a moment. 'So you understand, right?'

'I'm not sure I do.'

'Guys like you and me...sure, there's the job. We love the fight. It's what we do. We're set the task, and we execute. Simple.'

'Sure,' Grant agreed.

'Except it's not that simple. Is it? A samurai has honour. A code. They called it the code of Bushido. The way of the warrior. This isn't just about vengeance, is it? You think that you can bring back honour. Well, I hate to tell you, sunshine, the world doesn't care about honour. Not anymore. It's just about survival. And whoever lives the longest wins.'

Grant didn't reply.

'You should walk,' Faraday said. 'While you still can. We were both lucky to survive tonight. I can't make any guarantees about tomorrow. The only thing I know for sure is that we need to get that bullet out your stomach. After that is anyone's guess.'

CHAPTER TWENTY-SIX

They came off the A9 and pulled into Aviemore at the foot of the Cairngorms.

Grant had passed out a few miles earlier, the codeine kicking in to full effect. As Faraday took them along a winding narrow B-road towards the tiny village of Boat of Garten, Grant didn't stir once.

They pulled up outside a small cottage on the outskirts of the village, set back a short distance from the River Spey. Isolated from traffic noise, it was an oasis of calm after a stormy night.

Faraday dragged Grant out of the car, draping Grant's arm over his shoulder and walking him inside the cottage. 'You still with me, Duncan?' Faraday asked.

Grant's eyes fluttered, and he groaned something.

A woman Faraday's age – early fifties – was waiting, arms folded against the cold and light drizzle that had just started.

'Are you set up?' Faraday asked.

'Ready,' the woman replied.

'Good, because we're losing him here.'

The woman ran over, and slapped Grant gently on the face. 'Duncan, can you hear me?'

Grant fell into Faraday's arms, his eyes completely closed now.

The woman said, 'We have to hurry.'

The cottage looked modest on the outside, but inside was a different matter. The decor was modern, with lots of high-end electrics including a home cinema system in the living room, and an audiophile speaker set-up with a record player. One wall was lined with LPs, another with books.

Everywhere was tastefully lit. Photoshoot-ready. Down to the tasteful LEDs that illuminated the spines of her books.

The kitchen was equally well-equipped.

But it would be a while before Grant saw any of it. He was whisked straight to a large bathroom, where the woman had set up a reclining chair covered with a blue medical sheet. Next to the chair a scalpel, forceps, a clamp, a sponge, medical thread, and needles were laid out on a clean cloth.

The woman prepared the tools with urgency, readying the scalpel. 'Quickly down, Robert. We don't have much time.'

Faraday carried Grant over to the chair and laid him down, then he wiped nervous sweat from his forehead. Faraday had been out of the game for too long, and the events of the night had now caught up with him. He was easily the most anxious person in the room. When he saw how worried the doctor was, he knew Grant was in real trouble.

The doctor adjusted her rubber gloves as she inspected the wound.

'All right,' the doctor explained, 'listen to me, Robert. I don't think we have time for anaesthetic, and he seems to be out...'

Grant's eyes fluttered again, this time staying open. 'What's…happening,' he croaked.

Faraday looked with concern at the doctor. 'What do we do?'

'We have to go anyway,' the doctor said, swabbing the wound with alcohol. 'You'd better hold his hand. This is going to hurt.'

Faraday clasped Grant's hand. 'Hey, Duncan…' He leaned over, making eye contact. 'This is Florence. She's a doctor. She's going to get that bullet out, but there's no time to sedate you.'

'Just take it out,' Grant groaned.

Florence stared ominously at him. 'Duncan, it's not going to be easy but–'

'Just do it,' Grant insisted. 'Pain's in the mind. I can control my mind.'

Florence nodded at Faraday, who tightened his grip on Grant's hand.

'Okay,' Florence said, 'I'm making the first incision.'

As the scalpel gripped the skin then slit it apart, Grant gritted his teeth as the pain burst up his spine and exploded through his central nervous system.

The amount of blood seemed to take Florence by surprise.

'Robert, grab a sponge from the tray and soak up as much blood as you can. This is worse than I thought.'

Grant cried out, his vision going blurry. His brain felt unmoored in his head, like something floating on water. He could feel himself drifting.

The sponge that Faraday was holding was saturated with blood within seconds. 'What do I do?'

'Get another one,' Florence snapped, trying to concentrate on the clamp in her hand. 'Right, Duncan, we're nearly there. I can see the bullet. But it's lodged quite deeply.'

'Just cut in deeper,' he told her. 'I can take it.'

'I can't do that,' she replied. 'It's too deep for the scalpel. All I can do is pull. But it's near a nerve, okay. So this is really going to hurt. I need you to hold on.'

Shit, Grant thought. *Like it hasn't been hurting already...*

Florence inserted the clamp and pushed the broken flesh apart, wider.

Grant yelled in pain, his entire body rigid with tension now. 'Pull it out! Just pull it out!'

Florence got the clamp set around the bullet, but as she tried to pull it out, she lost her grip. When the clamp snapped shut, it drove the bullet deeper against the nerve.

Grant's vision went from blurry to razor sharp and blinding white in an instant. He thought he was actually levitating above the chair, the pain was so intense.

Florence blinked hard, knowing the pain it must have caused. 'I'll go again. Hang on...' She got hold of the bullet again with the clamp, this time with a firmer grip.

Grant gritted his teeth again, praying that she would be successful this time. He let out a series of small grunts, clinging on and clinging on.

Then with a final definitive tug, Florence pulled the bullet clear.

As it came free, blood poured even faster than before from the wound. Florence dropped the clamp and the bullet onto the tray, and pressed two sponges against the wound. 'Hold these tight,' she told Faraday.

Grant sighed in relief, allowing his body to finally relax. He sank back into the chair. The last thing he heard before passing out was Faraday's voice.

'Sleep well, mate. We're not out the woods yet.'

CHAPTER TWENTY-SEVEN

When Grant came to the next morning, it was daylight outside. The sun gently penetrating the light curtains. He winced as he turned on his side. He pulled the covers down, revealing a bandage – a proper one; not just a Tesco one – stretched over the bullet wound. It felt different there now. A few timid prods revealed that the bullet was out.

He tried walking a few steps, and was surprised to find that he was okay on his feet.

On the bedside table near the door, there was a small plate with the bullet that had been removed from his stomach. A note had been left next to the plate:

DO NOT REINSERT

Grant shook his head, wondering whose curious sense of humour it belonged to.

He followed the faint sound of Charles Mingus's classic jazz album *Pre-Bird* coming from the living room.

Curled up in a lush, soft armchair was the woman who had greeted them the night before.

'Sorry...I, eh...' Grant looked around, then back again. He squinted. 'We met...last night, didn't we?'

'You could say that,' the woman said, putting down the book she had been reading and removed her reading glasses. 'I'm Florence. A friend of Robert's.'

Grant felt at his stomach wound. 'You're the one who took the bullet out?'

'That's me.'

'Thank you,' he said. 'I don't remember anything about it.'

'You were pretty far gone when you got here, but I gave you a little something to keep you out during the procedure.' Once she'd had a drink from her steaming cup of coffee, she held it aloft. 'Can I get you one?'

Grant nodded enthusiastically. 'That would be great. I know it's bad to say it, but I often go to bed already looking forward to having coffee in the morning.'

Florence went about making a coffee from an expensive machine that wouldn't have looked out of place in Starbucks. 'I know what you mean. I'm nocturnal, so I get through a fair bit of it.'

'Is that nocturnal through choice or...' He trailed off, unsure if he was about to tread on something delicate.

'Not exactly,' she said, pressing the tamper down onto the coffee grind. 'I was a medic. SAS.'

'Is that how you know Robert?'

Florence paused, looking momentarily over her shoulder. 'You know, you must be the first person in years who, after finding out that I'm a medic and my name is Florence, doesn't immediately comment about Florence Nightingale.'

Grant shrugged. 'I tend to arrange thoughts in my head like a deck of cards. There's one in front of another. And to be honest, the card that finds your name amusing is quite far at the back.'

Florence went back to the coffee, intrigued by her strange guest. 'Robert and I met in Egypt. He was working, I wasn't. But he needed help.'

'Say no more,' said Grant.

She smiled. 'After I served in Bosnia, I stopped being able to sleep. Hence the big TV and speakers. They get me through the night, then I sleep by day. Once I left the SAS, I went into private healthcare for a while...' she gestured to her surroundings, 'then here we are.'

'A medic on the black market.'

She handed him a fresh cup of the nicest-smelling coffee he'd come across for a while. 'It pays the bills,' she said. 'But I thought Robert was out.'

'He was. I sort of pulled him back. Unintentionally.'

'You should know, I'm out as well. Last night was a favour for Robert. Don't make me regret a favour, Duncan.'

'I don't know who or what you think I am, but I'm not here to cause any trouble.'

'I'll bet trouble has a habit of finding you.'

'What makes you say that?'

She snorted. 'I've met your type before.'

'And what type is that?'

She paused. 'Have you ever heard of a man named Adrian Carton de Wiart?'

'Seeing as I'm not even sure if that was a name you just said, I'll have to plead ignorance.'

'He was an officer in the British army,' she said. 'But not just any officer. He was known by another name. They called him the unkillable soldier. And not without good reason. He served in the Boer War, the First World War, the Second

World War, playing key roles in the Battle of the Somme, Passchendaele, as well as the Polish-Soviet war. During these wars, he was shot in the face, head, stomach, ankle, leg, hip, and ear. He was shot twice in the same eye on different occasions, eventually losing the eye altogether. And he also survived two plane crashes, escaped from a prisoner-of-war camp by tunnelling out…' she held her hand up to make clear there was still more to come, 'and when a doctor refused to amputate de Wiart's fingers which had become detached during the battle of Aras, de Wiart simply tore them off himself.'

Grant gasped, 'Jesus!'

'This guy was on another level,' Florence explained. 'He was born into the aristocracy, and went the full nine yards. Balliol College, Oxford. But when he was about to start training as a lawyer, de Wiart decided that he wanted to go off to fight in the Boer War, even if it meant falsifying his age. The guy didn't even care what side he fought for. He offered his services to the Boers *and* the British. The first his father hears about this is when de Wiart is shipped back, having been shot in the leg. That should have been the end of it. But de Wiart wasn't done. He demanded to be redeployed, and that was when he was shot in the eye. I mean, I could go on for hours about this guy. Suffice to say, his life can be summed up in one quote from him. When asked about the First World War, he said, "Frankly, I enjoyed the war."'

Grant shook his head in disbelief.

Florence added, 'The point of the story is that de Wiart didn't know when to stop fighting. It was in his blood. He couldn't help himself.' She locked eyes with Grant. 'Some people just need the fight.'

'Is that what you think about me?' asked Grant. 'I don't need the fight.'

'Then what is it you want? What battle brought you to my door in the middle of the night with a bullet in your stomach?'

'I'm going to bring someone to justice,' Grant said. 'The sort of person who always gets away with it.'

'So it's about justice. And you believe in that, do you?'

Grant paused. 'I don't know. I think so.'

'There was an old saying with some of the guys in the SAS. If there's any doubt, then there's no doubt.' She waited for the message to sink in, before adding, 'There is no justice, Duncan. And nothing you do will fix whatever's happened, or bring someone back. Do what Robert did: get out, and don't look back.'

CHAPTER TWENTY-EIGHT

Grant stared down into his coffee. He thought about Gretchen. And Kadir Rashid. And Miles Archer.

Florence said, 'But I can tell you're not going to do that.'

'I can't,' Grant replied.

Faraday suddenly spoke behind them. 'You should.' He was wearing a grey t-shirt soaked in sweat.

Grant turned around. 'You went for a run?' he asked in surprise.

'Calisthenics,' Faraday replied. 'I work exclusively on bodyweight exercises. No weights, kettlebells, or barbells.'

It apparently worked very well. Grant had been around a lot of guys who were in good shape. But in the cold light of day, Grant could see that Faraday was in incredible shape for his age. In the baggy jumper he'd had on the previous night, it was hard to tell. But in a tight grey t-shirt, Faraday's arms and chest were chiselled. He hardly had an ounce of body fat on him.

Faraday went to the kitchen and took out a glass for water. 'You work out?'

Grant replied, 'Every day. Though I think I might call today a rest day.'

Faraday gave him a wry look. 'There are no rest days.' He downed the glass of water in one go. 'What do you deadlift?'

Grant pushed his lips out while he thought. 'The big log on the beach near my cottage.'

Faraday laughed, telling Florence, 'I told you this one was practically feral.' He turned back to Grant. 'You're not like the usual MI6 lot, Duncan. I might be a Londoner, but my heart's northern. They didn't realise that about me until they made me an Albion. It makes it easier to survive, when you've already survived so much by the time you even start selection. The others got there and they weren't ready. Weren't hungry.'

'That's what I was trying to explain to Florence,' said Grant.

Faraday shook his head while he poured another glass of water. 'You want to go after them, don't you? Set the world to rights.'

Florence said, 'We were talking about de Wiart.'

'Oh yeah. The unkillable soldier. Thing is,' explained Faraday, 'de Wiart just wanted to scrap. He didn't want all this other stuff that you want. What is again that you want?'

'I want John Wark. And the Crown Prince Muhammad bin Abdul. The pair of them in custody for ordering the execution of Kadir Rashid. And for causing the death of Gretchen Winter.'

Faraday tilted his head in Florence's direction. 'Still believes he can win, eh?' He turned back to Grant. 'You can't win, Duncan. You've got to trust that I've seen enough to know that.' He held up a glass. 'You want one?'

Grant shrugged. 'Sure.'

Faraday poured him a glass of tap water. As he held the

glass out to Grant, instead of handing it to him, he let it drop straight down.

Instinctively, Grant snatched for it, catching the glass without spilling a drop.

Faraday flashed his eyebrows up, impressed. 'Told you he was good,' he said to Florence.

She said, 'Guys, I need to know your plans. And I need to know if someone is going to come here looking for you.'

Grant said to Faraday, 'You've hidden here before. How long for?'

Faraday paused. 'What makes you say that?'

'You know where the glasses are. Seven different cupboards over there, you went straight to the right one.'

Faraday grinned. 'Very good. I was wondering if you'd pick up on that.' He told Florence, 'We'll be leaving soon. It's not safe to stay here.'

'You have to tell me why this is happening,' said Grant.

'What's happening and why are irrelevant. We have to leave here. Every hour that we stay, they get closer and closer. We're good, but we can't match their resources. The fake plate helped us evade number plate recognition last night. But in a couple of hours, someone in the MI6 Crisis Suite's going to match up Tommy Bonnar's missing Land Rover with camera shots from the A9 right around the time they'd expect us to pass through. Bonnar was a mere diversion to buy some time. It doesn't get us all the way out. For that, we need to make more decisive moves.'

'Like what?' asked Grant.

'Overseas.'

'No. Not yet. I need answers. Like why are MI6 wiping out Albions?'

Faraday put his glass down firmly, irritably. 'Listen to me,

Duncan. You're used to a world where you go on the mission and make everything right. That world's now over. It ended last night when your own agency tried to kill you. I was out. And now you've dragged me back in. The fact that you saved my life last night is the only reason this is even a conversation right now. I have no idea why MI6 is killing off former Albions. And I don't care. All that matters is that they're not going to take me out. I've survived too much.' He shook his head. 'You have no idea the things I've seen. The places I've been to. I won't let that all be for nothing. I'm walking out of here in three minutes. I know what I'm doing. I know where I'm going. I saved your life last night. We're even. Okay? So give me one good reason why I should take you with me.'

Grant didn't have to think for very long. 'Because the people I think are behind this are driven to the point of madness. I've seen what they're capable of. The lengths they'll go to just to maintain their power.'

Faraday chuckled despairingly and wiped his face. 'Duncan, you're talking about going after the British Foreign Secretary, who has one foot in 10 Downing Street already, and the Crown Prince of Saudi Arabia.'

Grant nodded, as if it were simple. 'That's right.'

'And why would I risk my life again to help you with any of this?'

'Because you wanted out. Now that's been taken from you. Help me for another forty-eight hours and I'll help you get back out again. You can be a ghost again, like you wanted.' To hammer home the point, Grant added, 'You're already running, Robert. You might as well be running towards something.'

His objections faltering, Faraday sighed. 'If we were to do it, we would need help. Someone you trust beyond any measure.'

Without missing a beat, Grant said, 'That's easy. Leo Winston, my handler. But we have to find a way of getting to London.'

'I can get us there. But as well as someone you trust, I need to know who's helping Wark. Someone in MI6 was in a control room last night calling the shots.'

'That's easy, as well,' Grant said. 'And until last night, I would have trusted her with my life as much as Leo.'

'Who?'

'If anyone has answers about all of this it's Olivia Christie.'

Faraday turned to Florence with an ironic laugh. 'Great. So all we need to do is find our way into a city with more cameras than anywhere else in the world, and secretly interrogate the Director of MI6 without being arrested or killed.'

Grant nodded. 'That's about the size of it, yes.'

Faraday patted him on the arm cheerily. 'Okay, then. As long as we're clear. Let's go.'

CHAPTER TWENTY-NINE

THE HUNT HAD BEEN ongoing for several hours into the night, and the intensity gripping the MI6 Crisis Suite remained as pressing as the opening fifteen minutes of the hunt for Duncan Grant and Robert Faraday.

Almost every analyst in the room was on the phone, typing feverishly, or in some kind of urgent conversation with a colleague. GCHQ had been roped in by Christie, giving full access to their terrifyingly powerful network of telecoms. There wasn't a public camera, phone, or internet connection that they couldn't tap into. The whole country was wide open to MI6.

At the centre of it all was the ring leader. Olivia Christie. Towering above the fray, watching the team's progress with narrowed eyes. She knew that what was taking place in the room would go on to define the rest of her career. They were going to find Grant and Faraday, meaning Wark would be home free. Without the threat of scandal looming over him and a Prime Minister in terminal decline, then Downing Street was little more than an open goal for him. If, however, Grant and

Faraday found what Wark and Crown Prince Mohammad had worked so hard to keep buried, then it would be Christie on the chopping block before anyone else. Wark would see to that. Of that, she was in no doubt.

After checking the time, expecting it to be two hours earlier than it was, Christie paced across the room to the analyst liaising with police and MI5 personnel.

'Where are we on Thomas Bonnar?' asked Christie.

In a matter of hours, the analyst had become an expert on everything to do with Bonnar. Across a number of custom-built, in-house apps, the analyst had access to Bonnar's entire life. Everything traced through phone calls, texts, emails, bank statements, internet history. They had it all.

The analyst explained, 'We'd been struggling to connect the dots between Faraday and Bonnar. But I think the key is in Bonnar being a builder by trade.' He pulled up Bonnar's phone location data sent over by GCHQ's Domestic desk. 'Bonnar had privacy settings on. Quite a lot of them, in fact. Which in itself is a bit of a red flag. He left school at sixteen, been a builder ever since. He had very little online footprint. No social media to speak of.'

Christie could see it straight away. 'So why is someone like him so precious about phone privacy?'

The analyst gestured that he agreed. 'It made me wonder, had someone coached him to do that. Except, if you dig a little deeper, he left some apps running in the background. Stuff that even you or I probably wouldn't even notice. They acted as back doors into his location history.'

'We can get that?' asked Christie.

'GCHQ has a relationship with most of the major app developers at this point. They feed data to GCHQ almost live.'

Christie leaned down for a better view of the screen. 'What does the location data show?'

The analyst zoomed in. 'There's a lot of signal dropout, and we don't have great satellite coverage in the area. But there are regular trips to the Loch Naver area three years ago. Bonnar's bank records indicate a series of payments from offshore companies, which feed back about a dozen ways down the line to a Robert Blake.'

Christie's eyebrows lifted. 'That was the last identity we left Faraday with.'

'After a few years being out and probably convinced he was in the clear, he must have got sloppy with his tradecraft. The payments link to similar amounts that Bonnar spends on building materials around the same time. We have the VAT records from HMRC.'

'Bonnar built Faraday's cottage.'

'That's what I started with. It didn't take MI5 to crack Bonnar. I think he lasted a full six minutes under interrogation. He admits Faraday told he would one day wire him ten thousand pounds if he was willing to drive day or night to a given location in Scotland at a moment's notice should he be contacted.'

'What about Bonnar's car?' asked Christie.

The analyst pointed out a colleague next to him.

She leaned forward to tell Christie, 'When we couldn't land any national plate recognition hits on Bonnar's car – a green Land Rover Defender – we searched for images of vehicles in the local area that Grant and Faraday may have taken.' The analyst indicated the video wall, which filled with hundreds of thumbnail images of vehicles. 'These are all the hits within a reasonable radius of Faraday's cottage. We know from Bonnar's arrest that they couldn't have travelled further than Lairg in the agency Range Rover Bonnar was picked up in. We assumed–'

Her more senior colleague shot her a disapproving look.

She corrected herself, 'We believed there must have been a swap. Probably back at Bonnar's house.'

'Swap out the plates,' said Christie.

'Exactly,' the analyst said. She showed an image of Bonnar's Land Rover on the video wall then gestured for her colleague to take over.

'We searched through camera footage last night. It took a while, but we got a hit.' He put up a still image of Bonnar's Land Rover driving onto Kessock Bridge. Then a still of the car parked in Tesco Extra.

Christie moved closer to the wall for a better look. Tell me you're inside the shop.'

The analyst switched to video footage of Faraday wandering the aisles with a basket.

Christie pointed. 'Do we know what he's got in there?'

'We've just got the itemised list through now. He bought co-codamol, bandages, some bottles of water…'

'So one of them's injured.'

Winston, who had been listening in, suddenly spoke from the back of the room. 'Not Faraday. Look at his gait as he walks. Unencumbered. No limps, no signs of bleeding or discomfort. If he was bleeding badly enough to have to come off the road to buy bandages, he'd be more obviously in pain.'

Christie turned back to the analyst. 'What else was on the list?'

He browsed through it, then gestured that he had no idea. 'Kids' party cups, coffee filters…I mean, frozen peas?' He threw his hands up. 'I don't know.'

Winston looked on. 'He was doing a cold-water extraction.

To extract codeine from over-the-counter pain meds. Grant's hurt.'

'If he needs codeine, then surely that will slow them down for the next twenty-four hours.'

Winston bobbed his head from side to side, considering it. 'Maybe only twelve, depending how bad it is.'

'Then we need to move. Fast,' said Christie.

CHAPTER THIRTY

Crown Prince Muhammad bin Abdul woke up sideways across his enormous Alaskan king-size bed, which stretched out three metres by three. More than adequate space to fit the four naked blonde women he was sharing it with. They were all asleep, having had their fair share of champagne the night before. In Abdul's palace in the heart of Riyadh, champagne flowed like tap water.

The women had been sourced privately, and were on a rolling contract which paid them more money than they would ever see again in their lives. What they had to do for that money was also something they would never forget. There was a fascination – and exaggeration – in some Western circles about the prevalence of human trafficking blonde Western women to the Middle East. Though it undoubtedly happened, a man like the Crown Prince didn't have to rely on such criminal behaviour to source his women.

In the sort of elite circles he occupied, there were dozens of casting agencies who dealt with customers like Abdul and their specific 'needs'.

For the Crown Prince, it was always blonde, always American.

How long they stayed varied on how much Abdul liked them. But none of them had ever stayed longer than three months. There wasn't a woman alive who could keep Abdul's attention for longer than that.

The women were flown in from Los Angeles by Abdul's private jet, with nothing more than a passport and a phone on them. Abdul provided everything they would need. And they wouldn't leave the palace grounds throughout the entire employment.

He always treated the women the same. Polite and friendly at first. Almost to the point of shyness. But that all changed the first night he invited them to bed. That was when he showed his true colours.

It always shocked the women, the seeming correlation between a man's riches and his deviancy. The more money and privilege they acquire, the greater the sense of entitlement to treat people like objects. Play things.

Outside, the call to morning prayers rang out, rousing Abdul who groaned in response. He rolled over to the glass bedside cabinet, where three lines of the purest Colombian cocaine had already been prepared for him by his personal servant a few hours earlier.

Abdul hoovered up the coke, then wiped his nostrils. He had become so hooked on the drug of late, that it had little effect until he was at least five grams into the day. The first few lines were merely to get him out of bed.

Drugs were inevitable for someone like Abdul. With almost infinite riches, there are only so many boats you can buy. So many beaches to sit on. So many holidays to take. With infinite leisure came infinite boredom.

He sat on the edge of the bed, looking at the woman next to him with disgust. Just because they satisfied his every twisted demand didn't mean he respected them. They were just employees, after all. Only marginally above the many stuffed animals placed all around the palace: tokens from Abdul's many hunting trips around the world.

The woman turned slightly, hearing the prayer call. Her arm draped over Abdul's, landing on his wrist.

He whipped his hand away from under hers. 'Be careful of the watch,' he snapped. He stroked the Patek Philippe Sky Moon Tourbillon watch – which cost nearly $5 million – with the sort of affection and care normally reserved for a tiny baby.

His phone started ringing. When he saw the ID, he took the phone out of the bedroom before answering.

It was John Wark.

'What is it?' Abdul asked in English.

Wark said, 'We've got a bit of a situation over here.'

'We or you?'

Abdul walked through the palace towards the lounge area completely naked, despite there being numerous servants and cleaners at work. None of them so much as looked in his direction. Anyone who made that mistake once, wouldn't have the opportunity to do it a second time. Abdul didn't even notice they were there. They mattered as much to him as flecks of dust in the air, caught in sunlight.

He put on a silk robe, and took the glass of freshly squeezed orange juice that had been sitting out of the fridge for seven minutes.

If it hadn't been drunk by minute nine, a servant would put it down the sink, and pour another one. This cycle could go on for hours until Abdul got out of bed. And the servants never knew how early or late it would happen.

'What's the situation?' asked Abdul.

'Grant's on the loose.'

'How long?'

'Twelve hours.'

'Why does that matter? It's not like he can make it to Saudi Arabia in that time. I've dealt with him before. Ghazi will take care of him this time.'

'That's not the only problem.' After a long pause, Wark said, 'Faraday's with him.'

Abdul froze. His expression steeled. He slammed the glass down. 'What's he doing back on the scene? We got rid of him, didn't we?'

'I made sure he disappeared,' said Wark. 'But Grant's brought him back into the fold.'

'What happens when Faraday tells him–'

'He won't,' Wark assured him.

'He might.' Abdul paused. 'You better pray he doesn't.'

After he hung up, Abdul called Ghazi, his Head of Security and personal body man. 'Grant's in the air again,' he said in Arabic. 'We need to be ready for anything.'

CHAPTER THIRTY-ONE

FARADAY WAS DOING THE DRIVING, marshalling them down the M6 south, through the Pennines, staying within speed limits, and doing the driving equivalent of being a grey man: anonymous and drawing as little attention as possible.

Grant was in the passenger seat, combing through the phone that they'd taken from the ambush team's lead man.

'You've been at that thing for ages,' said Faraday.

'Shit,' said Grant, stopping at a message.

'What is it?'

'I know this number.' Grant showed it to Faraday. 'That's an extension for the Crisis Suite at Vauxhall Cross.'

Having been out of the game for a while, it took Faraday a moment to realise. 'That was no rogue operation. That was an official hit.' He flicked his head in the direction of the phone. 'What are his protocols?'

Grant shook his head. 'What do you mean?'

'Well, in my day, on an op like that, there's no facility for briefing or getting updated instructions live when you're boots on the ground. There's no time. And somewhere like that, very little phone reception. Op protocols are loaded in advance onto the phone. It gives you all your key objective and contingencies.'

'That seems a bit risky,' said Grant.

'So is sending in a black ops team to the Scottish countryside to assassinate two MI6 operatives.' Faraday reached for the phone.

Grant tugged it away. 'Just concentrate on driving. What am I looking for?'

'Seeing as we got the phone off him before the end of their op, it's probably still in an open tab.'

Grant flicked through the open tabs, stopping on a PDF satellite image of the cottage and surrounding area.

Faraday explained, 'If there was anything they were looking for, it will be marked on the map. Probably with codewords.'

Grant pinched the screen to zoom in. 'Hang on...Shit.'

'What is it?'

'AC one eighty.' Grant let out an exasperated sigh, and put his head back. 'That explains a lot. At least why they want rid of me.'

Faraday shook his head in confusion. 'What's AC one eighty?'

'A year ago, I was on my first major mission. It involved a rogue Anticorruption and Internal Affairs director named Imogen Swann.'

Faraday's mouth hung open. 'Imogen *Swann*? A rogue agent? Don't be daft.'

'She was up to her neck,' Grant assured him. 'There was an Anticorruption file number one eighty she had redacted and buried on the orders of John Wark.'

'What was in the file?'

'It was an HM Land Registry file purged from the official database. The unredacted file showed a list of properties bought by Thomas Logistics.'

'Who are they when they're at home?'

'An agency shell company used to control slush funds in and out of the Albion programme.'

'What does that have to do with Land Registry?'

'Registry files show whenever property titles are transferred, and it names the owners of the titles. AC one eighty showed that titles for dozens of high-end properties across London had been transferred from Thomson Logistics to another shell company that was owned miles down the road by Crown Prince Mohammad bin Abdul.'

Faraday's eyes widened. It took several seconds before he could speak. 'You're telling me that MI6 bought property for a Saudi prince by laundering his money through an illegal black ops slush fund?'

'Basically, yeah,' said Grant. 'Wark and Abdul had it all worked out. MI6 was technically the source of the purchases, which meant that the Land Registry files could never be disclosed.'

Faraday nodded. 'Of course. Official Secrets Act buries it. Otherwise it would be public record.'

'Exactly. All you would need to join the dots would be a few pounds to buy the file, and a few breadcrumbs to know where to look. Get that file into the hands of a good journalist, and they would have documented evidence of corruption at the very heights of MI6 and the British government. AC one eighty ensured that the Crown Prince's property listings could never be declassified.'

'But the Crown Prince has got more money than God. What did he need all the complicated financing for?'

'To hide the investment from his father. Which is ironic, because fast-forward a few years, and Abdul's father's throwing money at London, and he's not been shy about it.'

Faraday paused. 'Wait...you said about if a journalist got their hands on it...Are we talking about Kadir Rashid? Is that why he was really killed?'

'Yeah. Rashid had the file. Originally, the hit was farmed out to Albion. The job was given to Henry Marlow. But Marlow found Rashid's research and realised that Imogen Swann had sent him in not for government business. But to execute on behalf of a private business deal between John Wark and Abdul. God knows what Wark was paid for his part. Swann got her cut too, of course.'

Faraday took a few moments to catch himself up to their own situation. 'Hang on...if this is all about this AC one eighty file, it's still buried isn't it?'

'Olivia Christie made sure of that,' said Grant. 'She did it as a favour to Wark in order to get Albion up and running again.'

'Why would she let him get away with that?'

'Because she wanted Albion. But she needed Wark to sign off on it. Albion had ended badly with Marlow going rogue. No one wanted to hear about Albion, much less bring it back. Christie said it was about a greater good.'

Faraday scoffed. 'Yeah, right.'

'If AC one eighty were to get back into the public realm, it would torch her and Wark. The Foreign Select Committee would see to that for sure. If Christie can keep AC one eighty buried she saves herself and her own career, and Wark remains on the path to Downing Street.'

'But why the hell is she gunning for me now? And what about all the others? I've been retired for years. Why would I have a file like that?'

Grant shook his head. 'I don't know. But she's the only one who can tell us. Without Christie, we won't have any idea when or how this stops.'

THE MEN STOPPED in the early afternoon between the Lake District and the Yorkshire Dales at Tebay services, blending in with the mixture of families, tradesmen coming to and from cross-country jobs, and truck drivers.

While Faraday loaded up on coffees and sandwiches in the cafe, Grant bought a prepaid phone from WH Smiths in cash that Florence had given him. He went outside to make the one call he needed to make. It was an emergency messaging service that could be accessed at anytime, anywhere in the world when making phone calls wasn't possible or safe.

Grant dialled into his messaging service, and was told, 'You have one new message...' While it loaded, Grant checked all around for anyone suspicious but saw nothing. Then Winston's voice came on. 'Grant, it's Leo. I don't know where you are, I don't even know if you're still alive as I send this, but I hope to God you get it. I'm on the inside with Christie, but I'm having to keep my cards close to my chest. She's all in on killing you and Faraday, and there's not much I can do about it. She expects at least a little pushback from me. Anything less would be suspicious. But if I go too far, she might do something far worse than simply push me out. I'm going to give you a number that you can call Randall on safely...' Grant memorised the number.

At the end of the message, Winston said, 'I'm sorry about all of this, Grant. If there was anything else I could do to stop it, you know I would. But I'm going to get you out. I promise...'

Winston trailed off and, for a moment, Grant thought the message was over. When Winston spoke again his voice cracked. 'I know I fucked up last night. I'm sorry. But I've got a second chance now to put this right. And remember what I said, trust no one. There's no telling where else this one goes.'

As soon as the message was over, Grant called the number Winston had left. It rang for so long that Grant nearly hung up. Then came a frantic voice, out of breath.

'Grant?' It was Randall.

'Yeah, it's me,' he replied.

'Thank God.'

'No, he didn't really have much to do with it. Listen, I don't have much time. I need you to trace some phone information for me.'

Grant gave Randall a mobile number he had found on the ambush team leader's phone. 'Anyone you use to trace that number has to be airtight,' Grant said.

Randall replied, 'I know someone over at GCHQ. Rebecca Fox.'

All business, Grant asked, 'Tell me about her. How do you know her?'

Embarrassed to admit it, he said, 'We, uh, met at a Scrabble tournament last year.'

'Did she approach you?'

'No, we only got to talking when we were drawn against each other.' Randall chuckled. 'She kicked my backside. She forked the board with–'

'*Forked the board?*'

Forgetting Grant wasn't the sort of guy who spent several hours playing online Scrabble tournaments on his days off like Randall did, he said, 'Oh, sorry. It means putting a word down that opens two different areas of the board to stop your opponent blocking.'

Grant paused. 'Yeah, I shouldn't have asked.'

'Anyway, she killed me with a triple-word score on "gladiolus". Not that any of that actually matters. Then I was at GCHQ for a conference, and she was there. We stayed in touch, and she owes me a few favours now.'

'Good,' said Grant. 'Because what I'm asking is going to require cashing all of those favours at once.'

'What do you need?'

'Every message and call from the last week, in or out. She can't know it's from me, and she can't know what it's about.'

Randall sucked in air. 'That might be tricky.'

'I wouldn't ask if it wasn't important, Randall.'

'No, sure.' His tone shifted to something more determined. 'I'll make it happen.'

'Is Leo with you?'

'No, he's inside Crisis with Christie.'

'Tell him we need to meet. Face to face. I'll message the time and location.'

Worried Grant was about to hang up, Randall said, 'Hang on, hang on, Duncan…Are you okay?'

The question took Grant by surprise. Randall sounded genuinely worried. 'I'll be better when this is all over,' Grant replied.

While he was taking the call, Grant didn't notice was Faraday inside by the amusement arcade, checking on Grant's position. Seeing that he was a distance away across the car park, Faraday took the drinks holder and paper bag of takeaway food over to a public phone near the toilets.

Faraday set down the coffee and bag, and popped some

change from the coffee shop into the phone. He dialled a number he had memorised for exactly his situation.

'Hey, it's me,' he said in hushed tones. No one responded, but Faraday knew they were there. 'We're coming to London. Grant knows it's about AC one eighty.'

A male voice replied, 'Does he know where it is?'

'No. But he wants to get to Christie to find out. You should make arrangements.'

The man at the other end hung up.

Faraday went quickly out to the car park. 'Sorry,' he told Grant. 'Queue was a nightmare. We should hit the road, partner.'

Grant got back into the car, oblivious to what he had missed.

CHAPTER THIRTY-TWO

Christie was personally checking each potential hit on a car for Grant and Faraday. She didn't want to miss even the slightest detail. And that went for events happening inside the Crisis Suite too.

She had been keeping a close eye on Winston anyway. But a series of minor events caught her attention. She'd seen Randall answer the phone, and within a few seconds had backed away from the bank of analysts' desks he was near. He then left the room altogether – which would have been strange enough in itself. As a tech and forensics expert, Randall wasn't often required to take phone calls on a national security level. And even if he had, there would have been no safer place to take the call than the Crisis Suite. Which told Christie that he didn't want anyone there to hear what he was talking about.

Then, when Randall returned still clutching his phone as if he'd only just hung up, he went straight to Winston and whispered something in his ear. Whatever Randall had said made Winston react with what appeared to be alarm or intrigue. Or both.

Christie had seen enough. She leaned down to a senior analyst and beckoned him over to a quiet corner. 'Are you up to date with your grids?'

'Yes, ma'am,' he replied.

'I need you to do something for me. It has to happen very quietly, and very quickly. Find out who Randall was just talking to on the phone. And I want every message and notification that comes through.'

'Yes, ma'am,' he said again, before scuttling back to his desk.

Christie folded her arms, watching Randall and Winston continue talking.

CHAPTER THIRTY-THREE

The Crisis Suite had been running all night, through the morning, and into the afternoon in the search for Grant and Faraday, and they somehow appeared to be getting further away from finding them.

Christie, who had been surviving thanks to a steady flow of black coffee and losing her temper at least once every hour, tried to reengage the team. She stood at the centre of the room and raised her hands for quiet.

'Okay, everyone, listen up. Down tools. Unless you're talking to Grant or Faraday, phones down, eyes up.' She took a deep breath, turning around slowly to speak to each team member directly. 'I want us to reboot here because we are...' she checked the time on the video wall, 'coming up on thirty-six hours in, and our two targets are still in the wind. Desk one, I want you on airports. That's our priority. If they leave the country, we're dead. A pair this good, we'll never see them again. Desk two, public transport. If they're travelling, I want to know where to. Desk three, I want you on Grant and Faraday's files. These are STRAP Two eyes only. If you need the clearance, raise your hand and I'll key you in on your screens. I want their past identities turned inside out. Anything that was left off Faraday's channels when he was active. Known associates. Safe houses they could be using. I want it all. And I want it yesterday.' Christie raised her head as she received a wave from a technician by the Crisis Suite door. 'And I want everyone drinking water at least once every hour. The biggest cause of brain fog in this job is dehydration.'

When she reached the technician at the door, he didn't say anything. And she didn't have to say anything either. The grave look in his eyes was enough to tell the story.

They went down the corridor to the far end, and went into a dark office. There was one other technician in there already, wearing headphones. He was frantically writing while he listened to something.

On a widescreen in front of them was Winston and Randall's entire lives encapsulated on an MI6 program. They had windows open doing live monitoring of their bank accounts, phone, email, home computers. They had it all. If a hair on their heads had moved, the two techs would have known.

'What have you got?' Christie asked, almost afraid to ask.

The other tech, standing, explained, 'We've been up on them for the last hour. Randall got a text from a prepaid phone a few minutes ago.' He tapped Tech Two on the shoulder. A text message appeared on the widescreen.

Trafalgar Square. 5pm. Leo alone.

Christie asked, 'Do we know the location of the sender?'

'Just leaving Birmingham.'

'Christ...they'll be in London in a few hours.'

'What would you like us to do, ma'am?'

'Stay on Randall's phone. Give me everything. I'm going to

get you moved to another room where you can liaise with a Survey team.'

'A Survey team?'

'Yeah,' said Christie, turning for the door. 'We're going to end this before tonight.'

When Christie returned, she noticed Randall showing Winston his phone. He thought he was doing it discreetly, but his lack of tradecraft or awareness of who was watching him was starting to show.

Winston walked casually past Christie, pointing towards the blackout room. 'I need to get some air,' he told her.

Christie approached Randall, who almost jumped when he realised she was crouching next to his station. 'How are you holding up, Randall?'

He drummed his fingers on his desk, trying to be casual. 'Oh, you know. Just getting on with it.'

'I know this must be hard for you,' she said. 'I know you and Grant were close.'

'Were?'

'Nothing's going to be the same after this, Randall. He won't be coming back. We need to be professional about that.'

Randall nodded swiftly. He tried to make as much eye contact as he could, but her eyes had a way of piercing right through him, as if she could see into his soul. He felt like the fact that he had been secretly communicating with Grant was screaming from every pore of his body. That Christie could tell just by looking at him. He tried to remember Grant's advice, to carry yourself with total confidence, even if what you're doing is a lie.

Randall said, 'He's gone too far this time. I blame myself. I really do.'

'People change, Randall,' Christie said. 'It's not your fault.'

She glanced towards the door. 'Do you know where Leo was going?'

Suddenly, with one question, all of his confidence shattered again. His nerves radiating, almost glowing out of him. 'I, uh... that, he...I'm not sure, ma'am. Maybe a cup of coffee?'

Christie stared at him. Then she patted the desk affirmatively with her hand. 'Keep up the good work, Randall. This will all be over soon.'

He tried to smile. 'I really hope so.' It wasn't a lie.

She stood up, then pretended to have just remembered something. 'Oh, could you grab me a coffee outside? Or get Leo to bring me one back?'

Randall paused, but there was nothing else he could do except agree to her request. Anything less would raise an eyebrow.

The moment he left the room, Christie buzzed the security guard outside, telling him, 'We're locking down in here for STRAP Three clearance.'

The guard locked the door from his computer, sealing the door. No one could get in now without the proper clearance. Clearance Randall didn't have.

Christie went to the front of the room. 'People, what's about to happen is going to happen quickly, and we need to be ready for anything. This is a Yellow Status situation. I have a source that says Duncan Grant is going to be at Trafalgar Square at five o'clock today. That gives us just over an hour to prepare. You guys are the smartest people in the building. That is why you are here. I need you to act like it. I want everything we have on Trafalgar Square. Every bus, every camera, and I want satellite on overhead. This could be our last chance. Let's not blow it.'

CHAPTER THIRTY-FOUR

In the car passing through Milton Keynes, Faraday eyed the sign for London. 'You're absolutely sure about this?' he asked.

Grant said, 'Randall's smart, but he's not street smart. Christie will have been watching him more closely than usual anyway. Randall and Leo are the closest thing I have to family. And if they were out in the real world, Christie would have Survey teams all over them. She would have noticed him taking the call, and there's no way he wouldn't give himself away somehow.'

'And you said you *wanted* him to do that?'

'If we're going to get Christie looking where we want her to, yes.' Grant looked across to Faraday.

He was shaking his head slowly.

'You think it's a mistake?' asked Grant.

Faraday chuckled ironically. 'The assassination of Archduke Ferdinand that started the First World War. Inventing dynamite. Chernobyl. These things were mistakes. What you're suggesting...' He trailed off purposely. 'I don't know what to call it. Suicide?'

Grant replied, 'I wouldn't go that far.'

'You want to go into Vauxhall Cross – MI6 headquarters itself – to break into Olivia Christie's office, while they're in the middle of a national manhunt for us both.'

Grant thought it over. 'Seems about right.'

Faraday nodded. 'Just checking.'

CHAPTER THIRTY-FIVE

THE CRISIS SUITE was in the full grips of operation prep. In many ways, prep was more frantic and urgent than the op itself. By the time an op is up and running, it's already too late to change the fundamentals. But failure to prepare was to prepare to fail.

There maps of the area unfolded across a desk where analysts combed over Tube routes, assessing which route connected to which and from where, and what station exits might be in play. Bus timetables were just as important, but trying to work out which ones Grant or Faraday might target based on the timing of their arrival would be difficult to figure out. Especially given the traffic situation in the area, which was of constantly gridlocked, where it was a fight to get through cracks in the traffic to advance even a few metres.

Christie took on board all their suggestions and guesses, but ultimately it was her calls that they would follow. For the first time, the fact that none of them were actually acquainted with Duncan Grant and his abilities was proving a hindrance.

Shaking her head irritably, Christie explained, 'Grant isn't going to get a bus to Trafalgar Square during rush hour. And he's not going to sit around on a bench waiting for Leo to show. He's going to be constantly moving, and we have to find him when he does. If we lose him for a second, that's all he needs.'

'Should we be worried about Leo's safety?' someone asked.

'We've got armed officers en route,' Christie said. 'He'll have full coverage.'

What Christie neglected to tell them was that Leo didn't know that anyone else was wise to the meeting.

A logistics analyst told Christie, 'Ma'am, honestly, I don't know if we can keep him safe out there in the circumstances. It's a surveillance nightmare. It's going to be busy, with a lot of people standing around in groups. Then you've got fountains, statues, street furniture to aid with concealment, and multiple staircases and balconies...'

Christie snapped, 'It's not our choice where the meeting is happening. We have to work with what we've got. This is it. Let's deal with it. And get me the Met Commissioner on the line. He needs a heads-up what's about to happen in the most tourist-dense area in his city.'

Someone asked, 'What about SFOs? Marksmen?'

'Not a chance,' Christie replied. 'Grant and Faraday together will be able to spot marksmen on roofs. And the whole point of Specialist Firearms Officers is that they're bloody visible. Neon, for god's sake.' She paused, considering the live CCTV shots of the square currently beamed onto the video wall, showing the place rammed with tourists and people leaving work for the day. It was only going to get busier over the next hour. 'No,' she said, 'if this goes south, all the police will be good for is mopping up.'

She leaned down to her own computer screen, which showed camera footage of Winston leaving Vauxhall Cross in a hurry. Unaware he was being watched from above, and on the ground.

The Street Team were some of the best the agency had at their disposal. A mixture of standby operatives, and others roped into duty while back in London for debriefings or HR meetings. Standby operatives were overlooked because they spent so much of their time doing other things at Vauxhall Cross. They were the designated fire officers of the espionage world. Their role was largely in name only, knowing the chances of them ever being called on for actual duty was slim to none. But when a job came up, it was critical that they were competent.

It was an occupational hazard that standby teams were only ever called on under extreme circumstances. Which meant that they were going up against intimidating, much more experienced targets.

One by one, and a few pairs, they filed out of Vauxhall Cross, managing to move quickly and efficiently without appearing to be chasing to catch Winston up. Their attire was more thoughtful than the typical black puffy jackets and jeans that persisted on TV shows and movies. One was dressed in a smart suit and carried a briefcase. They were a mixture of ages and genders, running the gamut from early twenties to late sixties. All of them wired into the Crisis Suite.

A suite that Randall was currently failing to re-enter. He argued his case to the security guard who repeated his protocols that only STRAP Three staff were permitted inside. Giving up, Randall set off for the exit, hurrying down the stairs.

A move that Christie was soon made aware of.

'Where are you going, Randall?' she wondered aloud.

Randall upped his pace to a run, stumbling as he lost his footing on a stair, then hurried out onto Albert Embankment.

'Will I have someone pick him up?' asked a tech.

'Give him a few more minutes,' Christie said. 'I don't want him alerting Grant yet.'

IT WAS a forty-minute walk to Trafalgar Square from MI6 headquarters. The fastest route straight along Albert Embankment next to the Thames, over Lambeth Bridge, then through Millbank, past Big Ben, the Cenotaph, Downing Street, and the Ministry of Defence. But Winston was barely aware of the landmarks' existence as he power-walked, and occasionally jogged, towards the destination.

His mind was a fog of fear and anxiety. Not just for himself, but for Grant as well. Depending on what happened out there, Winston would be limited in what he could do for Grant. The real joker in the pack was Christie, though. Of all the people in play, she was the one whose actions he couldn't predict. Not even a few months ago, Christie would have moved heaven and earth to protect Grant. Now she was hunting him down like a wild animal.

BACK IN CRISIS, the latest offering going around was a mock-up of Faraday's face. The last personnel photograph MI6 had on record for him was nearly twenty years old. A tech had been artificially aging him, doing mocks of four different versions of how he might look now. Variations of facial hair and hairstyles, that made him look like entirely different people in each one.

'They're ready whenever you want them, ma'am,' the tech told her.

'Not yet,' said Christie. 'I don't want anything circulating until we know what the shot is here. Is it on the network yet?'

'Not yet.'

'Keep it that way,' she replied.

The tech exchanged a confused look with a colleague. 'Ma'am, are you sure you—'

Christie barked back, 'If you think that the sort of person who needs an E-FIT to identify Robert Faraday or Duncan Grant is capable of either restraining or putting them down, then you have no idea who we're dealing with here. Until we know what they want with Leo, I'm keeping their faces off the network.'

Christie had come to the decision as a matter of instinct. But it was a decision that was about to have deadly consequences.

CHAPTER THIRTY-SIX

There hadn't been time for Winston to grab a burner from his office, so he had to buy one on the move. A purchase that Crisis saw happen from a street camera high above Parliament Square: one of the most intensely monitored pieces of real estate in the country.

Winston had Grant's number memorised, and there was no need to continue doing shoulder checks. He hadn't been active in the field for a long time, but all the old tricks and instincts don't leave an experienced spook like Winston easily.

Grant answered on the first ring, sitting at the back of a bus approaching Trafalgar Square. 'You're early,' he said.

'I'm not there yet,' Winston answered. 'I've got a tail.'

'Can you lose them?'

'I don't think so.'

Grant thought it over. He had prepared for the scenario.

'We should abort, Grant. There will be teams crawling all over the square by the time we get there.'

'Negative,' Grant said. 'The standby team's half its regular size. They're away training in Kent for another two days. In any case, what they want is me or Robert put down. They'll need to get close first. Christie won't risk marksmen, because she knows we'll spot them. She won't want to scare us off. Not when we're this close. And even if she kept them hidden – which she couldn't – no marksmen would take a shot from distance into Trafalgar Square. It would be like a darts player hitting a bullseye from fifty yards away.'

Winston was feeling unwell. A combination of the pain meds leaving his body from the night before, and not eating properly all day. Sleep deprivation was catching up with him too. He had been up the whole night along with Christie. Now his eyes were burning all around the lids, and he could feel them wanting to close. Yet at the same time adrenaline was rushing through his body, insisting that he stay awake to get the job done. 'Where do you want me to go?' he asked.

'The King George statue,' Grant said. 'Have some change ready. Please help. Don't judge. God bless.'

He hung up.

Winston took the phone down from his face to check if Grant was still there. Baffled by the cryptic instructions, he shook his head.

CHRISTIE KEPT CHECKING HER WATCH, comparing it to the time on the wall. 'Five minutes to go,' she said.

The team gave her a rundown of everyone's position. Some of the standby team had been given lifts in cars to get to the square faster, while a few straggled behind, staying within eyesight of Winston at all times.

Christie radioed the Street Team. 'How's it looking down there?'

Street One replied, 'Not great, ma'am. We've got porous sections on the north, south, and west sides and we don't have the bodies to plug them. There are too many souls in the square, and we need eyes on them if we're going to find Grant.'

Christie considered the options. 'Forget the perimeter,' she instructed them. 'Stay within the square's boundary. Prioritise face-checks. It's the only way we find them.'

'We're sure they're both there?'

'Two decades out of show business, there's no way Faraday would miss this. In any case, Grant would have demanded the help. He needs Faraday.'

'Roger,' Street One confirmed, then shook his head.

It was hard to imagine a worse scenario for trying to find someone. It had been unseasonably warm and sunny, and the square was packed with tourists, as well as locals. Tour guide groups were everywhere, streaming out of the National Gallery.'

'Shit,' Street Two muttered to Street One. 'What the hell is going on?'

'It's nearly closing time. Plus you've got commuters going home, and then there's the England game tonight. Short of New Year's Eve, Grant couldn't have picked a better time.'

It was like trying to find a single face in the middle of a crowded open-air concert.

Winston arrived soaked in sweat, his heart racing from the fast pace to get there in time, and the dense anxiety that was clouding his mind. He flicked his head from one direction to the next, hoping to find evidence of a Street Team. But in a situation like his, everyone he looked at over the age of eighteen appeared to be a possible Street Team agent.

It was a struggle to reach the King George statue at the back of the square, where the crowd was densest, congregating on the stone stairs: one of the few places available to sit.

Winston got up to the back level where the King George statue was, then he noticed a man sitting on the ground with an old baseball cap on the ground. The man had on a wooly hat, and was sitting on a tattered blanket. A small sign written in black marker on some old cardboard read,

"Hungry and homeless
please help
don't judge
God bless."

If Winston hadn't been given the instruction, he could have stood within metres of the man for minutes before even occurring to check the man's face – such was the prevalence of homelessness in and around central London.

Winston approached slowly, playing with some loose change in his hand. He dropped it into Grant's cap, then said quietly, 'What now?'

At a regular speaking volume, Grant said, 'Don't whisper. It draws attention. Look around. Absolutely no one is looking at us.'

Winston looked around. 'Where's Faraday?'

'Don't worry about that.' Grant got to his feet, and led Winston towards the back of a group of tourists, appearing to be part of the group. 'We don't have a lot of time.'

'Then get to the point.'

'I want you to phone Christie. Tell her to come down here. I'm ready to negotiate.'

'What are you, crazy?'

'She and Wark might be willing to do anything to bury AC one eighty, but I think even she would draw the line at shooting me in broad daylight in Trafalgar Square.'

'AC one eighty? Why do you think this has got anything to do with that?'

'One of the operatives she sent in to Faraday's cottage to kill us, we took his phone. Christie wanted him to check if Faraday had a copy of AC one eighty on the property.'

'But why would Faraday have a copy of that?'

'Exactly. There's something about the Rashid job. There's more to it than what we've been told.'

'You trust Faraday?'

'I wouldn't go that far. But for the moment, our interests in staying alive are shared. That's why I want to talk to Christie here. If I come into Vauxhall Cross they'll black bag me.'

'You think they won't black bag you here?'

'No. Not in front of hundreds of people all live-streaming or doing video calls. Unless Christie wants an illegal rendition all over the internet and on every newspaper cover tomorrow morning.' Grant held out his phone to Winston. 'Make the call.'

IN THE CRISIS SUITE, Christie and everyone else were scouring cameras for any sign of Grant.

Christie rhymed off the Street Team one member at a time, asking for confirmation of any visual. But they were all negative on Grant, Faraday, or Winston.

Christie sighed in irritation, then snapped her fingers at a tech. 'Get me standby. It's time to pull Randall in and see what he knows.'

RANDALL WAS RUNNING ALONG MILLBANK, trying to catch up with Winston. He had no idea what he was going to do once he got to Trafalgar Square, but he didn't get a chance to find out.

A plain white van pulled off the road and onto the pavement, blocking the way forward. Randall turned and ran – straight into the arms of a standby operative he had no idea had been following him the whole way. Randall kicked and fought, but the standby operatives were far stronger than him. Within a few seconds he was bundled into the back of the van, which took them back to Vauxhall Cross.

CHRISTIE RADIOED the standby team leader in the van. 'Get his phone. I want to find out if he knows an exact location–' She broke off, interrupted by a tech holding a phone out to her.

'Ma'am,' he tried to say.

Christie spoke over him. 'I need an exact location for Duncan Grant.'

The tech spoke more insistently. 'Ma'am, it's Duncan Grant. He says he's with Leo Winston.'

Before accepting the call, she pointed frantically towards the phone handset.

A tech was already booting up a trace. He made a circular motion with his hand, gesturing for her to draw out the length of the call so they could pin down his exact location in the square.

'Grant?' Christie said.

'I want to talk. You and me. King George statue...'

The techs put out the radio call to everyone.

In the square, all eyes turned towards the statue.

Grant went on, 'And if one of your guys comes near me and Leo, I shoot him right here.'

Christie stepped in quickly. 'No, don't do that, Grant. If you do that then we'll have nothing left to talk about.' She motioned towards the door to let the techs know she was leaving. 'I'm on my way. I'll be there in ten minutes.'

'Make it five.' Then he hung up.

'Don't worry,' Grant said, showing Winston the gun tucked away under his jacket, pointing at Winston's torso. 'It's just for appearances for the Street Team.'

Winston looked around nervously. 'Yeah, it better be.'

CHAPTER THIRTY-SEVEN

CHRISTIE BOUNDED DOWN THE STAIRS, flanked by standby operatives who had just returned with Randall in tow. 'You two, come with me,' she called. 'I think Grant's going to talk.' She pointed to Randall, 'You can wait in the blackout room. And have a think about the career you just flushed down the toilet.'

The standby operatives hustled Christie into the white van, which promptly sped off.

'Get me as close as you can,' Christie directed. 'I'll handle the rest on foot if we hit traffic.'

Back at the entrance to Vauxhall Cross, another operative – similarly dressed as the others, wearing a black hoodie under a brown pea coat – smoothly inserted himself into their slipstream.

'Hey,' Faraday interjected, tapping one of them on the shoulder. 'I'll take him from here.' He extended an arm to guide Randall inside.

The other operative hesitated, unsure about letting go. But everything about Faraday's demeanour and appearance seemed legitimate. The nature of the standby team meant that they were a revolving door of various departments. The fact that few of them ever actually worked together until thrown into an op was something that Faraday was only too happy to exploit.

Randall resisted at first, attempting to pull his arm away, which prompted Faraday to intervene. He took control of Randall, roughly, and in the process pulled off the operative's barcoded ID pass.

Seamlessly, Faraday pocketed it. Randall spotted the snatch and locked eyes with Faraday, who nonchalantly winked back. Randall squinted in confusion, wondering what was going on, but he said nothing – waiting to see how the situation played out.

Meanwhile, the operative had no idea what had just happened right under his nose.

With a smirk, Faraday told him, 'Feisty one, isn't he? Look, I'll take him upstairs if you want to crack on. Christie's got the whole place on edge with this whole Trafalgar Square op.'

Though a sliver of doubt lingered, the operative reasoned that if Faraday wasn't legit, then the secure entry at reception would expose him.

At the reception, Faraday made sure to be first to approach the desk. He oozed calm confidence, like someone who belonged there. It was a desk he had visited hundreds of times in his career, and knew exactly what to say. Apart from the control phrase that standbys were given in order to confirm they were entering the property safely, and without any duress.

Without Grant's recent knowledge of the system, Faraday wouldn't have been able to pull it off.

'Saber,' Faraday announced, looking calm and comfortable, which was easy for him to fake. The task that was still to come would have reduced most operatives – retired or not – to quivering wrecks.

This was the point where Grant and Faraday's plan would have fallen apart had Christie given the go-ahead for Faraday's E-FIT to be transmitted to the agency network.

Instead, Faraday was buzzed through reception like any other employee.

He scanned the barcode on the operative's pass, then intentionally loosened his grip on Randall's arm.

Feeling the pressure ease, Randall yanked his arm away again – just as Faraday intended.

In the minor ensuing scuffle, Faraday whipped around, pretending that Randall had hurt him. While he faked nursing a sore arm, Faraday slipped the man's barcode pass back onto his magnetised waist clip. Again, none the wiser for the sleight of hand.

Faraday made a show of shaking his arm off, then reasserting control of Faraday. 'Bloody hell,' he said, passing through the security scanner. 'I might take him to a quiet room upstairs first, if you know what I mean.'

Reacting to the scuffle with Randall had diverted the receptionist away from noticing that the same operative had scanned in twice within ten seconds.

Now he had passed through security like any other operative, the standby agent relaxed, convinced of Faraday's legitimacy.

But with nothing more than a little tradecraft and a little luck, Faraday was now within the hallowed walls of MI6.

And the tricky part hadn't even started yet.

Faraday took Randall towards the lifts. 'What floor's Christie's office on, mate?'

Randall did a double-take. It wasn't the friendly tone he

expected from a standby operative who had just detained him. 'Excuse me?' he said.

Still comfortable, and showing no signs of not belonging there, Faraday let go of Randall's arm.

Now in close enough proximity to him for no one else to hear, Randall asked, 'Who are you? Really?'

'Duncan says hi,' said Faraday, watching the LED screen for the lifts. 'What floor's Christie's office? I don't have much time, Randall. Quick.'

CHAPTER THIRTY-EIGHT

Grant saw Christie approach from a distance away, as she was flanked by two heavies from the Street Team.

'Go,' Grant said to Winston. 'Now.'

Winston did as Grant said, drifting back into the sea of tourists. He spotted a red hat on the ground that belonged to someone from a tour group who were all wearing the same hat. Winston popped it on and immediately became just another figure to dismiss on the Crisis Suite cameras.

Grant had his hands in his pockets, and made it plain that Christie had a gun pointing at her.

Remarking on the bulge sticking out of Grant's jacket pocket, Christie said, 'I better not get to the end of some devastating incriminating confession, only to find out there's nothing more than a pointed finger in there.'

Grant showed the pistol he was holding. On loan from Florence – though he wasn't sure if he would ever be able to return it to her. 'We don't talk anymore, Olivia.'

'That's Director Christie to you,' she replied.

'You're nothing to me,' he said. 'Ever since you set a wet team in after me and Robert Faraday.'

'You killed MI6 operatives.'

'I seem to recall *them* firing first.'

He shook his head in disgust. 'What did I ever do to you, other than deliver every single time. You send me out into the world, and I swallow the sins that you tell me to swallow. I swallow them because I believe that someone has to do that job, and it might as well be me. I did it to make the world a little more just. A little more honourable. And at the drop of a hat, the moment your career's threatened by a corrupt politician, you sell me out.'

Standing her ground, Christie leaned in. 'A convenient version that leaves out you shooting Henry Marlow for nothing other than revenge. Without anything resembling rules of engagement.'

'Rules of engagement! Is that meant to be funny? You ordered that wet team to take me and Faraday out so you could secure a copy of AC one eighty.'

Christie paused, running through in her head how Grant could possibly know about that.

'Yeah, I know,' said Grant, then felt his phone buzz with a message. Keeping the screen shielded from Christie, he read it quickly.

"RECEPTION"

Wondering what the message had been, Christie shot one of the team a knowing glance. The operative nodded, already on it.

Word came back quickly from the Crisis Suite that Grant

must have changed his phones. They weren't up on it and didn't know what message had come through.

Grant closed the message, then held his phone out. 'Don't you really struggle with reception out here at times?'

Christie squinted. 'I've never had bad reception here. What are you talking about?'

'Doesn't matter.' Grant pocketed his phone again. But while his hand was in his pocket, he navigated blindly to the share option for the audio clip he had just recorded.

IN CHRISTIE's office back in Vauxhall Cross, Randall was keeping watch outside her door. Meanwhile, Faraday crouched in front of a safe hidden behind a hinged wall panel behind Christie's desk.

When the message from Grant came through, Faraday played the attached audio clip, holding the phone up the safe's voice receiver.

An LED screen on the front asked for the control word – a randomised word from a dictionary list of thousands – which showed it as 'RECEPTION'.

Christie saying the word had been recorded just about cleanly enough to be accepted. The safe door released with a gentle click, then fell open.

There were only two items inside. One was a photograph of Christie's deceased mother and father, and a USB stick attached to a small black box. Faraday recognised it from the unique scanner on the side as a retina box. A secure method of portable data. Without the relevant retina scan, the USB wouldn't be readable.

Faraday removed it carefully like it was a bomb. 'Is that you AC one eighty in there?' he wondered aloud.

Randall opened Christie's door to give a frantic warning that someone was coming.

Faraday shoved the retina box into a backpack that Randall had found for him, then they hustled quickly out into the corridor.

Walking towards them were three men and a woman in smart suits who looked like they were from legal.

Without missing a beat, Faraday laughed the moment he opened Christie's door, as if he was in mid-anecdote to Randall. '...and that started a whole other thing, because we're stomping around Vienna without a map, and no one knows...'

The woman slowed and the rest of the group did the same. She pointed to Christie's door. 'Is she in?'

'No,' said Faraday, feigning frustration. 'I wait three weeks for a meeting with the director, and she doesn't show.' He led Randall as quickly away as he could without raising suspicions.

Even still, the woman peeked inside Christie's office, giving it a long look around from the door. But the safe was closed up behind the wall panel as usual, and nothing looked out of place.

When she closed the door, one of the older men in the group was still watching Faraday.

'Funny,' he mumbled.

'What?' asked the woman.

'I thought I recognised him from somewhere. From way back.' He shook his head as if it didn't matter, and he would remember it later.

At the far end of the corridor, Randall asked, 'What do you want me to say when everyone gets back?'

Faraday waited as long as he could tolerate before doing a shoulder check. The group had gone to the lifts, and were apparently uninterested in pursuing them. Faraday said, 'Tell them I left you outside the Crisis Suite, and you didn't know who I was. Trust me, the receptionist and the standby agent are going to get a lot more shit than you.'

Randall replied, 'I find that hard to believe.'

CHAPTER THIRTY-NINE

Christie inquiry hung in the air. 'So what now?'

Grant looked across the square, feeling his phone buzz discreetly with two messages back to back. He didn't have to look at them. Two empty messages signalled Faraday's safe exit.

Grant found it hard not to smile faintly.

'What's so funny?' Christie asked.

'If I told you, you wouldn't laugh,' Grant replied.

'What will it be, then, Grant? A nomadic existence like Henry Marlow's? Or perhaps you'll tread the path of a mercenary? Working in the shadows, risking life and limb for even less money than you make at MI6.'

Grant responded firmly, 'If that's the cost of doing what's right.'

'And what is right, Duncan? Enlighten me. Because I'm confused. I resurrected Albion. I gave you what you wanted.'

'By burying the truth. And now look at all the dead bodies left behind because of it all. The corruption. The greed.'

Christie reminded him, 'We're not here to achieve perfection, Duncan. We leave that to the people who want cheaper petrol, then whine when we do favours for the countries controlling those resources. They don't want us to get involved in unnecessary wars, but protest in the street when we back a regional ally that keeps the peace. Everything has a price. And everything has a cost. And the cost of you killing Marlow before securing those MI6 funds sealed your fate. You made it impossible for me to get Wark on your side.'

'So staying in the hot seat. That was your price.'

'We all have our allegiances. Including you,' she asserted, extending a hand. 'It's time to come in, Duncan.'

Grant scanned the surroundings. 'You know, a better spy would have asked about now Robert Faraday's whereabouts by now. And questioned why this conversation didn't just happen over the phone – if I truly intended to surrender.'

Christie's unease grew. She waited for the penny to drop, but Grant said no more. She radioed back to the Crisis Suite. 'Hub, monitor perimeter cameras.'

'At Trafalgar Square?' came the reply.

'No, Vauxhall Cross. We may have a breach.' She turned to the Street operatives behind her, motioning for them to move in.

Grant smiled as he balled up the blanket by his feet, preparing the concealed gun in his pocket. 'There's nowhere I can't hit you, Olivia,' he said.

As the Street operatives got within a few feet, creeping forward slowly, Grant backed up a step. Then suddenly, seemingly in a genuine panic, he yelled at the top of his lungs, 'He's got a gun!'

He pulled his pistol out and fired two shots into the blanket.

The gunshots reverberated through the open expanse of

the square, their thunderous cracks echoing off the National Gallery's exterior, sending startled pigeons scattering into the sky.

Those nearest to the gunfire instinctively dived and crouched for cover, their reactions fuelled by adrenaline and fear. Amidst the chaos, there was little time to process what had happened. The shouts and shots ignited a chain reaction of panic and terror, the crescendo of screams swelling like a tidal wave, sweeping down the staircase, and engulfing the lower levels of the square. Without clear visibility visual of what had happened, everyone reacted to others' reactions, fearing the worst. It was a perfect storm to create a stampede.

In the ensuing melee, Grant skilfully manoeuvred, able to deftly get bodies between him and the Street Team. As one of them prepared to take a shot at him, Christie intervened, throwing an arm out at the weapon and yelling, 'No!'

Grant disappeared into the frantic scrum. People were running in all directions. Groupthink taking over. No one had actually seen a gunman, but they reacted as if it was a certainty that someone was on the loose.

While the Street Team set off in pursuit, throwing people aside, Christie radioed back to the Crisis Suite demanding help.

'We can't see a thing!' came the frustrated reply, as chaos filled every camera they had.

The radio was just as frenzied, crackling with frenzied voices.

'What just happened?'
'I can't see a bloody thing...'
'We need eyes on the ground...'
'We don't have them!' replied the operatives in pursuit.

Aware that standing out would risk exposure, Grant matched his pace with those around him.

With traffic paralysed, an escape on foot was the only viable option. Though some people had been so spooked by the reaction to the shots that they abandoned their cars. Some in the square had experienced firsthand the aftermath of a terror attack, and they weren't going to run the risk of being caught up in another.

As the panicked masses streamed across the Strand to get as far away from the square as possible, Grant seized the opportunity, using the pandemonium as cover. With swift and decisive action, he grabbed a motorbike rider and hauled him off with a few swift tugs, then jumped on the bike. The only people who really noticed were the rider himself, and the driver directly behind, who looked on in amazement at what they had just seen.

In a matter of seconds, Grant disappeared, mounting the pavement on the Strand to escape the gridlocked traffic, joining a throng of food delivery riders and couriers seeking refuge from the mayhem.

CHAPTER FORTY

In the open air, panic surged unchecked, spreading like wildfire through the Mall and Whitehall. Everyone was stampeding away as if trying to outrun a tsunami.

It didn't take long for Grant to realise that staying on the road wasn't an option, as he weaved in and out of the static traffic. Within a minute, helicopters would be overhead, dispatched from a nearby base at the docks.

His instinctual plan when he'd taken the bike was to reach Waterloo Bridge and cross the Thames to evade traffic on wider, faster roads. But his erratic riding drew the attention of a lone police rider responding to calls of a gunman on the loose.

Thinking he had his man, the cop stamped on his pedal and set off in pursuit, radioing to his control centre that he might have a visual on the gunman.

Spotting the officer in his mirror, Grant knew that his cover was blown. Evading detection was no longer a concern. All that mattered was taking the cop out of his comfort zone. And Villiers Street was the perfect opportunity.

Partly pedestrianised, the narrow lane posed a challenge

for vehicles – even motorbikes. Grant revved the engine and honked the horn, urging pedestrians to clear the way. But his manoeuvre quickly turned perilous when he had to screech to a sliding halt to avoid hitting a small child separated from his parents. Swerving sharply to avoid any further risks to the public, Grant veered onto an offshoot lane leading under a railway tunnel now lined with shops and bars.

The bike's engine roared under the low arches as Grant accelerated, the sudden burst of speed catching him off guard. Approaching a steep staircase, he accelerated, hurtling upward. At the top, a businessman engrossed in his phone stood in his path, totally unaware.

The man looked up, seeing the motorbike only metres away. With nowhere to go, he turned his back and braced for impact, crouching low as Grant opened the throttle, and soared over the man's head.

The engine over-revved while it was in mid-air before landing – the rear wheel barely grazing the man's back as it passed.

Grant landed safely on Craven Passage, barely avoiding the lamppost in the middle of the pavement. Then he was out onto Craven Street.

But the Street Team following police radio had taken the shortcut down a lane accessible only to pedestrians, cutting Grant off at the north end of the street.

Grant hit the brakes and did a tight turn to face the other way.

Two police cars were charging towards him from the south.

There was no time for hesitation. Grant swiftly turned and raced back down the stairs, narrowly avoiding a collision with the man he had nearly decapitated with the front wheel of a Honda motorbike just moments ago on the stairs. The man had only just composed himself after his close shave with the bike, when he had to throw himself aside to avoid Grant a second time.

'Sorry,' Grant called out on the way past.

Remembering the Charing Cross tube entrance at the opening of the arches, he sped towards it, then slid hard right into the station. Racing up the deserted escalator to the top, he abandoned the bike while it was still in motion, letting it topple over as he moved onto his next objective.

The fleeting temptation to remain out in the open was now gone. There was no way of avoiding the police. He didn't want to go down into the guts of London, but he didn't have a choice. What he needed now was to get out of sight of cameras.

It was no time for pleasantries. He pushed his way through the next escalator down, then at the bottom, he veered off through human traffic coming from a recently arrived train. Testing several unmarked doors along the wall, he finally found one that opened.

The darkness inside the maintenance stairs and absence of surveillance cameras offered a brief reprieve. However, back in the Crisis Suite, the techs had monitored his movements, relaying them to the Street Team.

If Grant had been impolite in the way he'd descended the escalator, the Street Team were positively brutal, grabbing people by their jackets and shoving them aside – actually hurting people in the process.

Once the Street Team were in the maintenance staircase leading down, away from the public, they asked for permission to pull their weapons.

Christie replied, 'If you have the shot, take it.'

CHAPTER FORTY-ONE

Grant sensed movement overhead as he looked up through the grated stairs, spotting one of them aiming. Bullets ricocheted off the metal, perilously close to Grant's head, sending off sparks all around.

Reaching the bottom of the stairs, Grant found the only exit locked. With no alternatives, Grant booted the door off its hinges. When he pulled it out of the doorway, he was immediately greeted with the screech of a tube train hurtling past on the northbound line. Grant had taken the tube many times, but it wasn't until he was standing less than a few metres from one running at full speed that he appreciated just how fast they went.

Thinking through the geography of the station above relative to the river, Grant turned left, running up alongside the track. There was little room to accommodate both him and a passing train – as he was about to find out.

The lights of an oncoming train quickly appeared, travelling on the southbound line. Grant backed up against the wall, pressing as hard as he could to make his profile as thin as possible. The train driver blasted the horn as his lights picked up the sight of Grant. Not that there was anywhere else for Grant to go.

He shut his eyes and hoped there was enough room. There was. Barely.

The rush of wind was so powerful it nearly pulled him off the wall and onto the third rail.

The danger wasn't over either once the train had gone. It left behind enough light for the Street Team to see Grant's murky figure ahead.

More bullets whizzed past Grant as he crouched for cover, instinctively covering his head – though it offered little protection against potential hits.

The tunnel returned to blackness again. The Street Team persisted in firing, hoping for a lucky strike. But Grant had jumped into the centre of the tracks to get a better surface to run on. On the smoother concrete, Grant sprinted at full tilt, his arms pumping as hard and as fast as he'd ever felt them. His muscles screamed in protest. He couldn't even feel his legs. His body was pumping battery acid through his veins.

As the blare of another train's horn pierced the air, Grant knew it signalled impending danger. The approaching northbound train's headlights would soon expose him to the Street Team's gunfire.

With the tunnel straightening out ahead, he had to make a split-second decision.

He spotted another maintenance door ahead, but this one was on the other side of the tracks. He could get to it, but if it was locked and he couldn't get it open, the oncoming train would obliterate him, as there wasn't enough room between the tube line and the wall for Grant to stand.

But by staying in the tunnel, he was also inflating his chances of being shot by the Street Team, who continued to close in on him.

To make matters worse, another southbound train was coming already. And judging by the speed of both trains, the southbound one was going to pass him first – which might have been the twist of fortune he needed in order to pull off the seemingly impossible.

Even the Street operatives remarked, 'He's not going to do what I think he is. Surely...'

They opened fire again while they could, more persistently this time, sensing that Grant was about to attempt the death-defying leap across the tracks to avoid not one but two oncoming trains.

He couldn't think about the gunshots behind him. Those were out of his control. His timing had to be perfect to jump past the southbound train, which would give him the cover from the Street Team's gunshots to open the maintenance door.

But the northbound train was coming up so quickly, there would barely be any time to get the door open.

As risks went, it was colossal. Again, it didn't feel like he had a choice.

He waited as long as he could before leaping over the tracks in front of the southbound train, then sprinted hard for the maintenance door.

A quick tug on the handle confirmed that it was locked. He stole a quick glance down the line at the oncoming train. He had less than five seconds.

But in his urgency to try the door handle, he had yanked it clean out of its socket.

He looked down at the handle in horror, then threw it aside.

He took a step back onto the tracks, to get far-enough back to generate the power necessary to boot it through. But the door was sturdier than the last. He couldn't make a dent in it.

He kicked with everything he had – the door wouldn't budge.

The train bearing down on him, Grant only had time for one more kick. He grimaced, giving it everything he had.

It still wouldn't open. Realising he was out of time, he pushed himself up hard against the door and braced for impact. He knew he had no chance. There wasn't nearly enough space. But there was nowhere else to go.

Then, with metres between him and the train, Grant suddenly felt the door behind him give way, and a violent two-handed haul on his jacket from the back.

Grant was thrown into the stairwell, the train inches from collecting him at the feet. He sprawled on the ground, trying to get his head around what had happened. Then he looked up and saw Winston holding out a hand to him.

'Come on,' he said, pulling Grant to his feet. He tapped on his earpiece that he'd taken before leaving Vauxhall Cross. 'The network doesn't change,' he told Grant. 'It was like listening to football commentary on the radio. Bloody exciting.'

Grant dusted himself down. 'Glad I could brighten up your day.'

Winston urged him up the stairs. 'Come on. There's a service tunnel out one floor up.'

'I need somewhere to lie low,' Grant said.

'Yeah, I've had an idea about that. Do you know where Faraday is?'

Grant smiled. 'I know where he's *been*.'

With the train gone, bullets rained down around the

doorway from the Street Team. But they didn't have an angle to get either Grant or Winston.

They had survived. For now.

CHAPTER FORTY-TWO

Christie and the Street Team returned to Vauxhall Cross like a sports team that had just been thrashed in their home stadium. Everyone walking slowly, heads hanging. Every few minutes Christie asked for an update from the Met which brought the same response: no sign of Grant, Faraday, or Winston.

Her phone was ringing persistently from the same contact, but she wasn't answering. She looked again on the off-chance it was someone else.

JOHN WARK CALLING.

Christie shook her head and put her phone away, letting it ring out.

After scanning through the security cubicle in Vauxhall Cross, the guard behind the desk stood up. 'Excuse me, Ms Christie,' he said.

Christie eyes were half-shut. Now that the adrenaline had worn off, her body was begging to shut down. She couldn't remember the last time she'd slept. Her head feeling like what she imagined it felt like in a microwave.

'What is it?' she asked.

The guard was holding a note. 'A Declan Pritchard left a message for you.'

Christie narrowed her eyes and stopped. 'Who?'

'Declan Pritchard.' He handed her the note in a sealed envelope.

She opened the envelope. The note inside said simply "RECEPTION". Her head still a muddle, she waved the note at the guard. 'Who the hell is Declan Pritchard?'

'He's a standby, ma'am.'

She looked again at the note. Now she remembered it. The way Grant had said the word. Now with the note, it was like a magician drawing attention to a trick he pulled on you earlier, that you had thought strange at the time, but had overlooked until now. 'Check your logs,' she said with utmost urgency. 'Do it now!'

Spooked about what could have happened under his watch, the guard pulled up the logs.

He had barely finished typing when Christie leaned across the desk and turned the screen towards her.

The guard began, 'Declan Pritchard. He scanned in at...' He froze as he realised his mistake.

Christie saw it straight away. 'And why exactly did Declan Pritchard scan in twice within ten seconds?'

The guard stammered, unable to summon a cogent reply. Then he turned around and handed Christie another envelope. 'He left you this as well.'

She opened the envelope. The moment she pulled out the photograph of her mother and father, she pointed at the guard's controls. 'Lock us down. Now!'

The guard hesitated. 'Ma'am, are you–'

'I'm codeword arclight. Crash the building now!' Christie turned for the lifts and ran, still holding the photograph.

By the time she reached her office, her heart was beating out of her chest. If someone had got into the safe, then surely the retina box would have been gone as well. It must have been Faraday. Somehow.

She fumbled with the wall panel, almost hyperventilating. Her fingers were shaking so much she kept striking the wrong numbers on the keypad. In a rush, she pressed the alternative authorisation button, which prompted her to say the passcode "OCTAVIA".

The first time she said it, the safe rejected her because of the crack in her voice. She cleared her throat and tried it again. This time it was accepted.

When she saw the safe was completely empty, she whirled around to her desk and swiped everything on it onto the floor. 'No!' she cried out, smashing her fists down on the table, as the full implications of what had been stolen revealed themselves to her.

Then her phone rang again.

JOHN WARK CALLING.

She dropped the phone without answering and put her face in her hands. It had taken her decades of dedication, hard work and sleepless nights to end up in that office. To a title that held about as much prestige as the British establishment could endow.

And in the last forty-three minutes, it had all fallen apart in front of her very eyes.

CHAPTER FORTY-THREE

Grant and Winston had fled central London on foot, emerging from the Tube network at a disused tunnel in Blackfriars. They stayed off the major roads, keeping to small suburban streets, which added significantly to their journey time.

Every car that approached from behind brought another spell of anxiety that it would be the one carrying operatives from Vauxhall Cross to bring them back in.

Avoiding CCTV was almost impossible. The only way to deal with it was to keep their heads down as much as possible and move quickly. It was a simple equation that the more time they spent in the open, the greater their chances of flagging on MI6's network.

Winston watched as a pair of men walked towards them. They had close-cropped hair, and simply functional clothing. They couldn't have looked more like operatives.

Grant and Winston said nothing, waiting for them to pass.

Once they were gone, Grant asked, 'What do you think Christie will do next?'

'She'll have to drop a net on the city,' said Winston. 'She won't like it, because it will mean going cap in hand to MI5 and the Met. It's like an elder sibling asking the younger ones to help with their homework. If MI6 has a rep for anything in the intelligence game, it's that it cleans up its own mess.'

Grant glanced at a shop window to their left. 'Three o'clock. Red Ford Puma.'

Winston looked to the shop window as well. After a pause, he said, 'No.'

It was a game they had been playing for nearly two hours now.

'This is like Kill School,' said Grant. 'Street exercises. Running surveillance. Countering surveillance.'

'Yeah, except if you lose you might die.'

'Bloody Ridley.'

'Did you know him well?' asked Winston.

'No,' said Grant. 'Apparently not.'

'Who do you think sunk their nails into him?'

'Christie, of course. She thinks she's going to be in the hot seat for the next twenty years. And she'd promise anyone anything to make it happen. Even cutting deals with John Wark.'

'You think he's behind all this?'

'Christie wanted a search done at Faraday's cottage for a copy of AC one eighty. We sat in a room together with Imogen Swann when she showed us the unredacted file. If it ever got out, Wark would be toast.'

'Faraday, though,' Winston began, sucking his top lip. 'I don't know...'

'You don't trust him?'

'Why would Christie even think that Faraday had a copy of AC one eighty?'

Grant did a quick shoulder-check as three young boys burst out a newsagent, shouting at each other before throwing down crackers on the pavement. 'There's something else we're not seeing yet. Whatever was in AC one eighty, can't be the full story.'

'There's only one man can fill us in on that.'

Grant checked his watch. 'And he should be at the safe house by now.'

'You said the safe house is Faraday's.'

'That's right.'

'Is it wise to go there before we know for sure he can be trusted?'

'We don't have much choice, Leo,' said Grant. 'All our safe houses will be crawling with operatives and surveillance by now. They'll have thrown a net over London twenty miles out from Trafalgar Square. They know public transport is out. And we've only got so many safe locations in the city.'

FARADAY HAD KEPT the safe house running for years now. Located in a high-rise in Tower Hamlets, it was an ideal scenario for a safe house. Crammed in between hundreds of other occupants, it was easy to flit in and out unnoticed by neighbours. And spooks by trade didn't enjoy working rougher areas. They tended to stick out more. One word out of their mouths, and locals knew they didn't belong there.

Grant and Winston ascended the stairs to the tenth floor. Taking the lift was too risky.

'We can't make much noise,' Grant said. 'Faraday said he hasn't been back here for a while. If the neighbours hear anything they might call round. You never know.'

Winston nodded in approval.

In the car park far below, there was a lot of yelling and aggression on display. Rival gangs passing through neutral territory.

Grant crouched by the door, removing the third brick from the right of the door, first row. He had hoped not to find the key because it would mean that Faraday was already there.

He reached in and took out the key. Showing it to Winston, he said, 'Damn.'

They went in quietly, Grant gently pushing the door closed to avoid it clicking.

He went straight to the living room and closed the curtains.

'He's late,' Winston said.

Grant checked his watch again. 'He's not that late.'

Winston didn't say anything.

Grant said, 'I know what you're thinking. Don't say it.'

Winston was a picture of innocence. 'I didn't say anything.'

'But you were thinking it. I could hear you.'

Winston scoffed.

'He's not been caught,' Grant said. 'And he's not dead.'

'It's just...a guy like that is twenty-five minutes late for a meet...' He bobbed his head from side to side. 'It's not looking good, Duncan.'

'It's five miles on foot, Leo. He'll be here. I'd rather he was late and safe than here and bringing a squadron of police with him.'

The flat was musty and thick with dust. The meagre light struggling through the thin curtains was enough to highlight every dust speck in the air.

As Winston sat down, his weight threw up a volcanic eruption of dust in the air from the overly soft couch. Recoiling, he covered his mouth and started coughing.

Grant shushed him.

'This reminds me of a safe house I visited in my early days,' Winston said. 'I was a junior on the European desk back then. We had an operative come back in from Hungary. I don't know what happened, but he'd ended up shot and stabbed. Somehow he'd made it home. The guy was something else.' He paused, shaking his head gently at the memories. 'It made me want to be like him. He seemed so...together. The dedication. The willingness to do whatever was necessary. I didn't think I had it in me.'

'But you did,' Grant replied.

Winston demurred. ' Maybe.'

'Leo, you were imprisoned and tortured for six months by the Chinese. Most people wouldn't have walked away from that. They would have spilled their guts after a week hoping for leniency. Then the Chinese would have sent them to a labour camp and shot them.'

Winston's expression shifted, the memories turning darker. 'It's true. I didn't know that at the time. That wasn't why I held out. I held out because I had been trained to hold out. But yeah, if I'd talked, they would have discarded me. Being "used up" they called it. I tell you, if you think MI6 disposes of their own, you should spend a few years with the Chinese MSS.'

'I hope that I've got your strength,' Grant said.

'And I hope,' replied Winston, 'that it's never needed.'

CHAPTER FORTY-FOUR

Olivia Christie dropped her keys in the porcelain bowl by the front door and let out a weighty sigh. It had been without question the worst day of her professional life – and possibly her life in general.

Her surroundings certainly helped ease the pain. She lived in one of the grandest, stately townhouses in Cadogan Square, Knightsbridge.

She kicked her shoes off, abandoning them on the doormat. It was going to be one of those nights, she thought. Work clothes off the second you arrive home. Hot shower, dinner, a few glasses of wine, to try and forget about it all.

That was the plan, at least.

She turned on the living room lamp, then gasped. She put her hand to chest, then released the air she'd just sucked up in a fright.

'Jesus,' she exhaled.

'Just John will do,' said Wark. He was sitting in an armchair, swirling a glass of whisky around. In a mock light-hearted tone, 'So, how was *your* day?' Before she could answer, he blasted on, 'Because I spent most of the evening talking the PM down off a ledge because the Home Secretary has had the Met Commissioner screaming at her, which means the Home Secretary has been screaming to the PM about me...' his voice built to a shout, 'because I'm responsible for running the shitshow you call MI6!' Feeling better now that he'd got it off his chest, he exhaled then raised his glass to her. 'This is my second,' he said. 'I hope you don't mind.'

'I hope you don't mind if I catch you up,' she said, pouring herself nearly a triple measure.

'Looks like you're trying to catch up in just one gulp. And I don't mean the whisky.'

Christie sat down on the couch opposite. 'It was a shitshow, from start to finish. They completely played me.'

If she had been hoping for a sympathetic audience from him, then Wark quickly dispelled that notion.

He said, 'In a way that I wouldn't have thought possible. Now you want the PM to mop up for you. Have you any idea the political capital that's cost me today?'

'I do.'

Wark took a sip of his whisky. 'No, I don't think you do. I had to get him to order a citywide lockdown across all our intelligence networks, all to capture two of our own. Not terrorists. Not gun runners. Not paedophiles or drug dealers. Two of our own. Three if you count Winston.'

'Yes, well, he's got plenty to answer for here as well.'

Wark leaned forward on his knees. 'I had to beg, Olivia. To that fucking...*estate agent*. That middle manager. That side-parting. Because he needed a reason for the lockdown, and we can't give the real reason. He can't know what's at stake.'

Christie necked a fair measure of her whisky, then screwed her face up at the harshness of the sting in her throat. 'All we have to do is get back the file, and get Grant and Faraday. If we get those, we're in the clear.'

Wark shook his head. 'They'll have had the file for hours, Olivia. Have you considered that there could be copies of AC one eighty being sent out to every major news network? Right now, as we speak? And do you understand what happens then? All of this: you, me, the Crown Prince, it all comes tumbling down. And at the centre of it all will be you sitting in front of a Foreign Select Committee answering questions about Albion on the fucking news.'

'It won't come to that,' said Christie.

'Really? Then how are you going to get the file back?'

She paused to think. 'We need to flush him out.'

'Marlow already killed the girl. Grant doesn't have anyone else.'

Christie finished her drink, then left her mouth open a little. Shocked that she could even suggest such a thing. 'Randall,' she said. 'He'll want to protect Randall.'

'Really? That's your plan? Cut off some agency dweeb's balls?'

'It's his weak spot. He wants to expose what happened with AC one eighty, but not at any expense. He wouldn't allow Randall to be hurt.' She took a deep breath. 'So that's exactly what we have to do.' She got up to pour herself another drink, letting the idea settle in Wark's head. Her glass refilled, she reiterated, 'We have to hurt him.'

Wark finished his drink and stood up. 'Whatever it takes. I've always said that. A lot of people say it but don't really understand what it takes. We can't flinch, Olivia. Not now. Not when we're this close.'

Christie nodded.

He laid his hands on her shoulders, keeping them there for

a moment. 'I know things are rough right now. But I promise you, they're about to get much better.' He walked towards the inner door in her hallway. He paused, pushing her shoes aside with his foot.

She opened the door for him. 'I'll be in touch.'

Without turning around, Wark said, 'Goodbye, Olivia.'

Christie stood in the doorway, then was blindsided by a man who had been hiding between the inner and outer doors. He was dressed head to toe in black and wearing black leather gloves. With a single thrust, he plunged a knife into her stomach.

Christie's eyes were wide with shock and a crippling agony that was beyond words.

She was looking right at Wark's back, begging him with her eyes to at least have the guts to watch. But he kept his back to the terrible scene.

The man held the knife in Christie's stomach, then used it to push her back inside to the living room.

Wark turned around just as the man kicked the front door shut. Wark stood there for a minute, listening to Christie's guttural cries – the last sound she would make before she died.

With a trembling hand he covered his mouth, then took a steadying breath. He whispered to himself, 'Things are getting better already.'

Once he was in his car downstairs, Wark shut the divider between him and the driver. He made a phone call that didn't even last ten seconds.

Wark said, 'I've held up my part of the bargain. It's time for you to do the same. Make sure Grant gets here.'

CHAPTER FORTY-FIVE

GRANT PACED AROUND THE FLAT, his nerves shredded. He had no internet access, and barely a view out of the living room window. All he had to link to the outside world was a burner phone and no contacts in it.

Winston emerged from the bathroom looking drawn and grey.

Grant had heard him throwing up several times, but didn't want to broach the subject of why.

Winston sat down with a groan and stared into space. 'Still no word from Faraday then?'

'Nothing,' Grant said, peeking out the curtain for a view towards the south London skyline dominated by Canary Wharf and the financial district.

Winston's phone pinged with a message. 'Randall,' he said.

'Where is he?' asked Grant.

'He's been banished to his office. Says he's expecting to be suspended before he goes home.'

Grant shut his eyes in dismay. 'I should have just walked away like I wanted.'

'I'm sorry,' Winston said. 'I know it's my fault...because of what I did. It probably made you stay.'

Without missing a beat, Grant said, 'Staying for you is the only good thing to come of this, Leo.' He paused. 'But I'm worried about your complexion. When did you last eat?'

Winston shrugged. He genuinely had no clue. It could have been five hours ago. It could have been twelve.

Grant could see his Adam's apple bulging from a hard gulp. *Here it comes*, he thought. The reason for the sickness and everything else.

Winston stammered, 'I, uh...I think...I could really do with a drink.'

Grant looked at him in disbelief. 'We're on the run from SIS, and you want me to nip out to get you a quarter bottle of something?'

Like any alcoholic worth his salt, Winston pressed on with all the justifications why he needed a drink. 'Just one, Duncan. To settle me down.'

'It's never just one, though, is it, Leo? That's the problem. You have to accept there's no other way for you to deal with it than to say no altogether.'

'It's not just about booze,' Winston croaked. 'It's about Faraday, all right. Randall's been doing some digging.'

'What did he find?' asked Grant.

'Access to his Albion files are sketchy, as you can imagine. His era was all pre-digitisation. But Randall's found some things...he's got a theory.'

'What's the theory?'

'That Faraday is working with Christie and Wark to destroy all evidence of AC one eighty.'

'That makes no sense,' said Grant. 'I barely saved his life in Sutherland. Those were real bullets being fired at him. It wasn't just luck that allowed him to walk out of there. I know what I saw.'

'And I know what Randall is telling me about Faraday's past. What he's shown me.' Winston stood up and presented his phone to Grant. 'That's a screenshot Randall took earlier in the records room.'

It showed one of Faraday's Albion reports, replete with an eighties-looking font, and stained, aged paper.

'Look at the signature,' said Winston.

Grant pinched the screen to zoom in. 'My God...'

The signature was a scribble, but the printed name underneath was in no doubt.

JOHN WARK.

Winston said, 'Faraday and Wark go way back. Randall's got a dozen of Faraday's files with Wark's name attached. He was his section chief, Duncan.'

Grant handed the phone back. 'They kept that quiet.'

'With good reason. Wark was summarily fired the same month that Faraday retired. Now that can't be a coincidence.'

Grant only had to think it through a few seconds before he was shaking his head. 'But why would Faraday be involved? AC one eighty is all about the Kadir Rashid hit ultimately, and the property deal that Rashid was about to expose. Faraday had been long gone from the agency by then. Wark was already Foreign Secretary! And in any case, it was the Saudis who hit Rashid.'

'Was it?' asked Winston. 'Who told us that to begin with?'

Grant exhaled with a dire expression. 'Imogen Swann. She fed us a story to keep us away from the last layer of the onion.'

'What if Faraday was roped in to carry out the Rashid hit when Henry Marlow flaked out? It makes perfect sense. They couldn't get a new Albion onto it, because it would be their first job. You don't throw someone into the lion's den like that. Not on someone unproven. And we know MI6 had a history of throwing agents into the role without them being ready. Look at the failure rate, for god's sake. Half of them died on the job.'

Grant said, 'But what about this thing Faraday stole from Christie's office today?'

'The thing that he's been alone with now for hours? He could have swapped it out, produced a fake, or removed anything incriminating. Whatever it is.'

Grant was starting to see Winston's side. 'If this is true then we should go right now. Why would we wait for Faraday to come? He's hours late as it is. The Met Firearms Command could be on their way for us.'

Much to Grant's surprise, Winston said, 'No.'

'No?'

'Keep your enemies closer, Duncan. You don't want a man like Faraday in the wind where he's free to plot against you. You need him close. You're smarter than him. You'll get him eventually.'

Grant paused, then nodded affirmatively. 'Okay, but if we're doing this, then you should go in.'

'Me?'

'You could claim that you haven't been with me. You've been hiding out.'

'Why would I go back in now?'

'That one call from Randall proves, I need someone on the inside to help me. Randall said himself, he's probably going to be suspended. If that happens, then I've got no one inside MI6.'

'Christie won't go for it,' said Winston.

'Then you're going to have to convince her.' He gestured at the dingy, smelly flat they were standing in. Look at where we are, Leo. We can't beat these people from here.'

'How are you and Faraday going to pull this off? What does Faraday even have in that retina box? It could be nothing.'

'It's possible,' Grant admitted, then he stopped. He moved quickly down the hall to the front door. He pushed the dusty lace curtains aside to see out over the balcony. 'Shit...'

Winston met him in the hallway. 'What is it?'

Grant ran to the living room window and was met with a similar sight. 'Shit,' he repeated. 'There's police crawling all over the place down there.' He ran back to the front door to get a better view of what was happening.

Police officers streamed out the back of vans, tearing up stairs and fanning out across balconies.

Grant's face was pressed up against the frosted glass. Then Faraday's face appeared on the other side. Grant jumped back and let out a burst of surprise.

Faraday tapped on the window. He whispered, 'Let me in, for fuck's sake...'

Grant opened the door.

Faraday was frantic, bursting through the door and marching straight to the living room window. 'Thank God for that,' he said with relief. He pointed down. 'It's just a raid on another flat.' He looked around at the sparse filthy flat. 'This place takes me back...'

Grant and Winston shared a cagey look with each other.

Faraday was carrying the backpack he'd put the retina box in earlier. He opened the bag and took the box out as if it might detonate.

'Where the hell have you been?' Grant demanded.

'Sorry,' Faraday said. 'I thought I had a tail. I couldn't come here until I was certain I'd shaken it.'

'A retina box?' asked Winston.

Faraday leaned down for a closer look, lusting after it like a collector eyeing up a new discovery. 'It's a retina box. The only way to access the data inside is a retina scan of the owner.'

'Who's the owner?' asked Grant.

'Christie presumably.'

'We don't know that for sure.'

'It was in her safe, Duncan. Either she can open it, or she can tell us who can.'

Winston asked, 'Why would she open it for us? After everything that's happened?'

Faraday said, 'Because if you're right about what's in AC one eighty, then it's bad for her, but it's worse for Wark. If we can convince her that it's in her interests to get out ahead of this, she might turn on Wark.'

Grant pursed his lips, unsure.

Winston looked similar.

Faraday said, 'Come on, Grant and I are a couple of fugitives. We need someone of her credibility in our corner.'

Winston admitted, 'It's possible.'

Grant added, 'She did stop the Street Team firing at me. She didn't have to do that.'

'I don't think she really wants us dead,' said Faraday. 'I think she's playing along to make it appear to Wark that she's doing everything she can.'

Winston deferred to Grant. 'It's your call, Duncan.'

Grant nodded once. 'Leo, you should go back to MI6. We might need you there. The longer you're out the harder it will be to come back in.'

'He's got a point,' said Faraday, then he turned to Grant. 'But we should talk to Christie.'

Grant and Winston chuckled.

'I'm serious,' said Faraday.

'What, just track down her address and knock on the door?'

Faraday paused. 'Yeah. Why not? She's a regular citizen like the rest of us.'

Winston, who had been in Christie's flat multiple times, could attest. 'It's well guarded by technology, but there's no security guards if that's what you're wondering. You'd be amazed at whose door you're free to go and knock on.'

Faraday said, 'We need to get into that box, Duncan.'

Grant relented, 'Okay. Robert and I will go to Christie and—'

'It needs to be her home,' Faraday added. 'If we go near Vauxhall Cross again it might be out of Christie's hands. Wark might have taken over by then.'

Grant turned to Winston to check.

Winston agreed. 'You have to try. Robert's right. And it needs to be tonight. The landscape could have totally changed by tomorrow.'

'Right,' said Grant. 'How will we get there?'

'Easy,' said Faraday. 'I've got a car downstairs. Let's go.'

While Faraday set off down the hall, Winston pulled Grant back.

'You be careful, you hear?' he said. 'If there's a hair out of place that you don't like the look of, you walk.'

CHAPTER FORTY-SIX

Faraday pulled up outside Christie's house in Cadogan Square, Knightsbridge, in a battered Fiat Punto.

'Not exactly incognito in a Punto around here, are we?' Faraday remarked.

Grant leaned over to see up to her window.

Faraday asked, 'How do you want to do this?'

'I'll go up. If it's clear, I'll give a signal at the window. No point in us both getting turned over if she's got any surprises waiting for us up there.' Grant hunted around by his feet, then in the back seat. 'Where's the retina box? If it's Christie's I want it open as soon as possible.'

Faraday reached under his seat and handed him the backpack.

Grant got out the car and headed up the stairs leading to Christie's building. He was in the middle of looking for the right flat to buzz, when the main door flapped open a little in the wind. Grant glanced back to the car, where Faraday was giving him a thumbs-up.

The staircase and building interior were palatial. He went

up the stairs quietly. It seemed like that sort of building, where any unexpected noise would be greeted with neighbours throwing their doors open.

When Grant reached Christie's door, he knocked on it gently. Looking in through the frosted glass, Grant felt like something wasn't right. No lights on for starters. Total silence. Still. If she was home, there should have been something.

He tried the door handle, turning it and found it unlocked. He checked behind first, then went in without a word.

Once he had closed the main door behind him, he didn't bother calling out Christie's name. He slid the backpack off and left it in the hall. All the other doors were closed, except to the living room.

Grant peeked in with half-averted eyes. Olivia Christie was lying on her back in the middle of the floor on an oriental rug, blood still pouring out of her stomach. There had to have been litres on the rug already.

A knife stuck out of her stomach.

Grant checked for a pulse, but it was a mere formality. No chance anyone could have survived such blood loss.

His shock at finding her dead body was soon replaced with horror when he looked again at the knife.

It was his.

The one he had looked for at the cottage before he was about to leave to track down Wark and the Crown Prince. He'd had the knife on him throughout his travels in previous weeks. There was only one person who could have stolen the knife.

Christie herself.

She'd been playing a long game, all right, thought Grant.

His theory was that Christie had taken his knife in order to set him up or to be killed himself. She had never thought she would be the victim in the set-up. Now she had ended up dead herself as part of the cover-up plan for whatever was going on with Wark – who was surely continuing the process of covering his tracks.

Grant came back to the present, retracing his steps on the way through. The knife told him he was being framed. He'd also just touched the front door handle to get in. So he quickly formed a list of tasks that had to be performed. He had to wipe the door handle, remove the knife, and get out of there. He counted himself lucky he'd got there before the police.

Which reminded him. Faraday.

He ran over to the window to give a warning signal. But there was a problem.

Faraday wasn't there. Up the road in the distance, Grant could see the Fiat speeding away between the long rows of parked cars on either side of the street.

Stunned and confused, he dashed to the hall for the backpack and threw it open.

Inside, was a small cardboard box, and inside…

Grant's heart sank. How could he have let it happen?

Inside the box was a tin of soup.

'Faraday, you…' Grant trailed off, more concerned about the flashing blue lights heading towards the flat.

It all made sense now. Faraday being the one to push going to Christie's. The weak excuse for why he was so late to the safe house. He could have been sitting around with Wark all that time.

The problem was that Grant had to leave immediately, and there wasn't time to do the clearing up he needed to do.

Leaving the backpack and the knife behind, he ran to the top of the stairs, but it was too late. Police officers were already filing up.

One noticed Grant standing in the doorway. The officer pointed, 'You! Stop...'

Grant threw the door shut, then went to a bedroom window. He had noticed it while Faraday was parked downstairs. It had become automatic, scoping out entries and exits on any building he went into.

Grant pushed the bedroom window up to open it. He stuck his head out and looked up. It wasn't great but it would have to do. He climbed out onto the ledge, as police sirens now wailed on the street outside. The blue flashing lights bounced off the surrounding buildings, creating a wall of light.

As Grant shimmied up the drainpipe attached to the wall, a neighbour opened their window and looked up at him. When she shouted at him, it alerted police on the ground far below to Grant's presence. Torchlights danced around him, warnings from the police rang out to come down and give himself up.

At least they aren't shooting at me, thought Grant.

The police kept their lights on him, but Grant was already at the top, and hauling himself over the top of the gutter onto the roof.

From there he had a perfect view of the scale of the police presence. And they were all oblivious to him up there.

Grant ran across the rooftops, the city lights flickering in the night as he sought refuge. But his fleeting sense of escape was soon shattered. His description had gone out over police radio. As he darted into the quiet side streets near Shaftesbury Avenue, every beat cop in the area was on high alert for anyone matching Grant's description.

It happened quickly: Grant locked eyes with a police officer standing at a corner, finishing a routine stop for drunk and disorderly. But when he recognised Grant, the cop simply abandoned the arrest and set off after Grant.

He tried to remain the grey man, but he had never felt so many things piling on top of him at once. Losing Gretchen, Winston's attempted suicide, the AC one eighty conspiracy, Christie's murder, and now his being framed for it...

The officer who had spotted him was still in pursuit. Then a passing police car prowled past to get a closer look at him. The driver hit the flashing lights, thinking it might intimidate Grant into giving himself up. But they had no idea who they were dealing with.

With desperation gripping him, Grant maintained a normal pace as long as he could, hunting for a place to hide, hoping he could still disappear into the crowd leaving bars and restaurants and shows nearby. It was hopeless. The police were onto him. Breaking into a sprint, he darted towards the crowded streets, the police in pursuit and calling for back-up. Despite their numbers, Grant's agility and determination gave him an edge, carving a path through the dense throng. But to get away for good, he needed to do something decisive.

In one last bold move, Grant bolted across the busy Vauxhall Road. A car screeched to a halt, narrowly avoiding him as he leapt across the bonnet and landed on the other side. But his escape was short-lived, as an oncoming food delivery rider, ignoring a red light, barrelled into him, sending him crashing to the ground.

Grant felt like he'd been hit by a train made of hammers. He lay sprawled on the ground, trying to gather himself. The sound of the approaching police encouraged him to shake it off, regardless of the pain in his ribs.

The collision sent Grant flying along the tarmac, as well as the rider. Grant thought about taking the rider's bike but it wasn't fast enough to make a difference. There were multiple police cars on the scene now. Which meant Grant had to go on foot.

He turned towards a staircase leading up and away from Shaftesbury Avenue but saw cops at the top of it. He turned around to find another route, and ended up walking straight into another cop. Grant sent him straight to the ground with some simple but well-practised arm twists, thanks to Grant's mantra he had coopted from Bruce Lee: "*I fear not the man who has practices ten thousand kicks once, but I fear the man who has practiced one kick ten thousand times.*"

The officer lay sprawled on the ground, groaning to himself.

'Drama queen,' Grant muttered to himself, then stole the officer's radio.

Listening to their updates on Grant's movements while appraising which route to take, Grant ran into the shadows of side streets with Italian and Chines restaurants. He put a call out on the radio that the suspect was heading north on Shaftesbury Avenue.

Meanwhile, Grant ran in the opposite direction.

As far as escape routes went, St James's park was close, but Hyde Park was a better option at night. That's when Grant remembered something from Henry Marlow's old file. He had once owned a lock-up from his early Albion days around there. Without a map or the internet on his phone, Grant was left to wander the streets checking street signs on each, until he found it.

Lismore Street.

The lock-up was in the old railway arches that had been

converted in garages, lock-ups and studios, all on a very grungy and poorly lit street.

Marlow's lock-up was shuttered but easy to break into. When Grant threw the shutter up, he couldn't believe how much gear there was. There were guns. Phones. Computers. All old but still working. And everything he needed to fight back.

CHAPTER FORTY-SEVEN

Grant took one of Marlow's old phones, plugging it into the wall to get a charge going – the batteries had run down on everything unsurprisingly. It had been years since anything had been switched on.

The laptop Marlow had used was still functional, though it had taken ten minutes just to boot it up.

Grant dialled into his emergency call service, which revealed he had one waiting message. But instead of hearing Winston as he expected, he found a call from Olivia Christie.

'Grant, if you're listening to this, then there's a good chance I'm dead. I know it might be hard to believe after everything that's happened. I pushed just hard enough to keep Wark at bay, but I knew between you and Faraday you'd find a way to escape. If I appeared weak or reluctant for even a second, I wouldn't have been able to protect you later as Wark would have removed me from the op already. You have one chance now, to take the contents of the retina box and expose Wark and the Crown Prince's collaboration in the Rashid assassination. When Wark reopened Albion, I didn't believe it wouldn't come with caveats. So I made a copy of the evidence in AC one eighty. The evidence that, if my suspicions are correct, have been stolen from you by Faraday. But Faraday doesn't know the whole story. He thinks the retina box only opens with a scan from me. Getting rid of me is convenient to Wark because he thinks it will secure the box. What he doesn't realise is this: the retina required to open the box is his retina, not mine. I stripped the bio-data from his personnel file months ago. Find the box, then find Wark, and you'll have everything you need to blow this sky high. I'm just sorry I won't be there to see you do it. Goodbye, Grant.'

Grant sighed and shut the phone off. He leaned over the counter and stretched out his back. He looked around properly, taking in the surroundings. It felt strange to be somewhere that Marlow had been. He was the reason for so many things in Grant's life. Marlow had changed everything. Now there he was, back where it all started in a way. A lock-up from when Marlow was an Albion – just like him.

It made Grant wonder about the choice he faced about what to do next.

The choice wasn't easy, but it was simple:

Walk away and spend the rest of his life hiding like Faraday, or risk his life to expose the truth.

He shut his eyes tightly, trying to wipe the image of Gretchen from his mind. But he couldn't. She was there and was never going to leave. Not until he had set things right. For her. For Rashid. And all the others.

When he opened his eyes, he saw a pop-up on Marlow's laptop. The MI6-coded VPN that Marlow had used to get the laptop online and access the MI6 internal network had updated and refreshed to the latest version. The resolution of the screen was terrible, but the interface and access were there.

Grant could now get into anything that someone in the Crisis Suite or the European Task Force could.

But after scrolling around the network, Grant realised that there was a list of recently viewed files stored on the network drive. It might have been a long time ago, but Marlow's viewing history was sitting there for Grant to see.

The last thing he looked up hadn't been Wark, or Rashid, or even himself.

It was Winston's personnel file. Specifically, the debriefing carried out following his release from captivity in China. Having checked the dates that Marlow had read them, they matched up with when he had taken Imogen Swann hostage. Winston would have been an unknown entity to Marlow back then, and he clearly had done his homework.

The debriefing report was stark, shocking, and graphic. Winston, of course, hadn't told Grant the half of it. The torture he had endured at the hands of the Chinese MSS was incredible. It was no surprise he'd turned to booze when he got back.

Grant's phone screen lit up, ringing on silent.

LEO WINSTON CALLING.

'Duncan,' Winston said in relief. 'Thank God you're all right.'

Grant leaned in, struggling to hear him.

Winston went on, 'I'm at Christie's and it isn't pretty.'

'Yeah, I know,' said Grant. 'I was the one who found her.'

Winston paused. 'Duncan, I don't say this lightly...but you need to come in.'

'The hell I am.'

'They found your knife here. It was the murder weapon. They've got your prints on the front door handle, and the police saw you climbing a drainpipe to escape. This is serious, Duncan. This is murder. This isn't just spy games anymore.'

'Yeah, I'm aware of that, Leo. I was aware of it when the police were chasing me through Knightsbridge and Covent Garden.'

'I thought you were with Faraday.'

'I was,' Grant said. 'Then he ditched me. He gave me a fake retina scan box. He must have kept the real one for himself.'

'I tried to warn you, Duncan.'

'Between him and Ridley, I'm getting the message that I should stick to working solo from now on.'

'Faraday doesn't surprise me,' said Winston.

'Christ, I really needed you the other night before Sutherland.'

'I know, Duncan, I'm sorry. But even if I'd been in a fit state to advise you that night, I wouldn't have been much help. I never knew Ridley. Never worked with him.'

Grant said, 'I should have trusted my instincts.'

'Look, Duncan. You need to come in and answer some questions about you and Christie tonight. At least allow the police to eliminate you from their enquiries.'

'Yeah, that's what will happen if I come in, Leo. I should never have come back in. I should have done the mission I had planned and gone after Wark and Abdul.'

'There's still time. If we can track down Faraday…'

'Faraday's in the wind,' said Grant. 'All he ever wanted was out. For good. Now he's got all the leverage he needs if the agency ever tries to mess with him again. He played this beautifully from the start.' He shook his head. 'I tried to do the right thing. To come back for the right reasons. But I know that the only way to end this is to become a monster like them. I tried to do it my way, but it can't be done.'

'What are you saying, Duncan?'

Grant paused. He turned towards the shutter door.

Shadows under the foot of the door, moving, shifting from side to side.

Grant didn't even want to whisper in reply to Winston. He hung up, then moved quickly towards the hard-case box under the counter that contained Marlow's old side pieces.

He picked out a Glock 22, the service weapon of choice for police officers abroad. He checked it was loaded, then slid in profile along the right-side wall, gun poised.

Throwing up the shutter to confront whoever was outside wasn't an option. It would rob him of positional advantage. At least in his current position, the suspect didn't know Grant was there.

They rapped on the shutter, then there was a gentle cry of, 'Grant, open up...'

Grant knew the voice. He backed up quickly and took aim at the shutter.

This was probably it, he thought. If he was out there, then there was surely an extraction team with him.

'Shutter's open,' Grant replied, re-gripping his gun. His eyes were wide, ready for the fight. He felt at peace, almost calm. If this was the end, it seemed as good a place as any to end it. Full circle in the depths of Henry Marlow's safe house, assuming his position of rogue operative, being hunted by his own.

The shutter went up, revealing Faraday standing in a supplicative stance. His hands were raised, palms showing. Going to great lengths to make sure Grant could see they were empty.

'I can explain,' he said.

The gesture meant little to Grant. Questions swirled in his head. Too many to think of which to confront him with first.

Faraday kept showing his hands. 'I'm unarmed,' he emphasised.

'I don't care,' said Grant, knuckles uncharacteristically white around the gun handle. Then, this wasn't any normal combat situation he had faced before. 'So you found me. I don't know how. Congratulations. But if you think this is going to end with me black-bagged and shipped off somewhere, you've got another thing coming.'

Faraday continued to keep his hands out. 'I know what you're thinking.'

'I highly doubt that.'

'If I was in your shoes there would be a couple of questions in my head.'

'Only a couple?'

Faraday's eyes were wide like saucers. Something about him was emitting honesty, openness. It didn't seem like an act.

But Grant told himself that it had to be, and that he couldn't allow himself to be tricked.

Faraday said, 'I would probably start with how did I find you?'

'A decent place to start.'

'Look under jacket collar.' He indicated where he should look. 'All you need is one hand.' He made a come-here gesture. 'You can keep pointing the gun at me.'

Grant felt around underneath his jacket collar. There was a little ridge in there. He pulled it out. Before he had got a chance to look at it, he knew what it was. He had handled them hundreds of times before.

Faraday explained, 'When you leaned over in the car to find the retina scan box.'

'You think tagging me proves that you're on the level.'

Faraday was relishing the opportunity to give his side. His

tone was verging on a plea. 'If all I wanted was to get you black-bagged or arrested, I would have just told MI6 or the Met, and this place would have been surrounded by a small army and you'd already be in cuffs by now. Why would I bother going through with this?'

Okay, Grant thought. A decent start, but he needed more. A lot more.

'What would my next question be?' asked Grant.

Faraday said, 'If all I ever wanted was to get out, why have I come back?'

'That a simpler one. I think you're up to your neck in this Rashid case. If you're working with Wark, delivering me would be a good way to prove your worth.'

'True. But again, if it was just about delivering you on a plate for Wark, why are we standing here talking? Because there's another question: if I'm on the level, why did I leave you in the wind at Christie's?'

'The question has crossed my mind a few hundred times tonight, I'll be honest.'

'When Henry Marlow bailed on killing Kadir Rashid, it left Wark and Abdul with a problem. Abdul wasn't willing to risk Ghazi, his most trusted associate. And Wark wasn't willing to risk giving the job to a new Albion. So they came to me, offering me one final pay day. I was thirty-six years old when I retired. What do you do for the rest of your life as a retired assassin at that age?'

'You killed Rashid?'

Faraday showed the first signs of cracking emotionally. Stopping well short of tears, but his emotions seemed genuine. 'They told me he was a bomb maker. He was living in Switzerland, and was a well-off Saudi national. There were no red flags for me going on. I never checked, I never asked questions.

That's on me. That's how I did it. It was the only way to do the job. Back then, we all trusted in what we were doing. If we were given a target, then it meant they must have done something pretty bad, or were planning to.'

'How did it work?' asked Grant.

'It was my job to set up the Saudis. You must have read about them during the Marlow op. They were low-level goons, barely a brain cell between them. They were all due big sentences at home in Riyadh, so Abdul offered to reduce their sentences if they were willing to do a job for him overseas. Of course they jumped at the chance. The rest was simple for me.' He broke off. 'When I saw who he was on the news, I freaked. I knew then that I was done. That I would never come back. These people...' He shook his heads. 'We're *nothing* to them.'

'You've been working with Wark since then?'

'No, he let me go. With Marlow in the wind, he had enough to worry about. He didn't want to make another enemy from the Albion programme. He was terrified of us. What we were capable of. Think about it: if I was working with them to try and track down AC one eighty to stop you getting it, why did they try and kill me as well at the cottage? You know that if you hadn't been there I would have been dead. They sent in Ridley to finish us both off.'

'You had a copy of AC one eighty? Christie seemed to think you did.'

'It was bullshit from Wark. He knew I didn't have any evidence other than what I could testify to in a court or a Foreign Select Committee hearing. He didn't send that team in there to rescue evidence. It was a hit on you and me, plain and simple. Two operatives who had full knowledge of what he had been up to with the Crown Prince.'

'Then why did you leave me at Christie's?'

'It had to look convincing, so that Wark would let me get close to him again. I swapped the retina scan box from Christie's safe and took the real one to him. To prove I was on his side.'

'For what purpose? I could have been arrested at Christie's. They've framed me for it.'

'All that was already in motion. There was nothing I could do to stop it. I couldn't control the evidence they had left behind incriminating you. And I knew you would be able to get away from a bunch of uniform cops. But being part of the set-up at Christie's proved my worth to him. I didn't know she was dead up there, Grant, you've got to believe me!'

'I really don't have to believe anything you say, Robert.'

'I admit, I wanted to steal the intel. The real retina scan box. But I didn't care about opening it. Not anymore than Wark did. Both of us, we just wanted rid of it to protect ourselves. I couldn't risk the last copy of evidence of my involvement in Rashid's assassination coming to light. Just look at what's been happening to SAS squaddies in Afghanistan. They shoot someone in a war zone, and they end being charged with murder.'

'They're accused of excessive force. Killing unarmed civilians.'

'Say they had, Grant. What about the country that sells cluster bombs to Yemen, a war we're not officially fighting. How many unarmed civilians are those killing? Thousands? Where are the murder charges for our Foreign Secretary on that? Wark was always going to walk away from this, but guys like you and me? We're never safe. The point is that I couldn't take the chance. I just wanted out, I admit that. I told you that from the beginning. But when I saw what Wark did to Olivia Christie, it changed me. This is my last chance now, to make amends. For Rashid. For Christie. And everyone else. You're right, Grant. They have to pay. They all do.'

Grant blinked heavily. It all sounded right to him. Maybe a little too right. 'It's a great story. I'm sure that I could have come up with some equally convincing versions of it all if I was in your shoes.'

'If you shoot me, Grant, we lose the last chance we have of setting things right.'

Grant still couldn't see the bigger picture. 'How are you planning on doing that?'

'Come with me,' Faraday said, waving him towards the shutter. Sensing Grant's reluctance, he reiterated, 'If all I wanted was to see you in cuffs or shot, why would I bother explaining all of this?'

Grant edged closer to him. 'Slowly. Open the shutter. Where are we going outside?'

'To my car.'

To Grant's surprise, his instincts were telling him that Faraday was indeed on the level. He pressed and pressed on each of his answers, but none of them failed to stand up to scrutiny. What Faraday had done all made sense in a way.

'Hands behind your back,' Grant said. 'So I can see them.'

Faraday kicked the shutter back up, just high enough for them to crouch under it.

Grant followed. As soon as they were outside, his eyes were everywhere. Picking out spots for a sniper. But it was deserted. Surely the quietest street in London. All Grant could hear was the steady dripping of a leaky gutter into a puddle below.

'Open the boot,' said Faraday.

Grant was still pointing the gun at his back, waiting for so much as a flinch from Faraday's hands.

'You do it,' Grant said. 'Easy, easy…nice and slowly.'

Faraday made slow, deliberate movements, opening up the boot to the Fiat. Once the boot door was open, he stepped back, showing his hands once again to Grant.

There was something moving around in the boot. Something dark. Feet? Legs?

Grant stepped carefully towards, expecting a shooter. Instead he found a man with a black hood over his head, his hands cable-tied together behind his back.

Now that the man could feel cold air, he was wriggling and writhing. Trying to shout, to scream. But his mouth was taped underneath the hood.

Grant motioned with the gun. 'Take off the hood.'

Faraday leaned over, being careful with his movements. He held the hood up. 'If I wasn't on the level, then why would I have come back to deliver this?'

Staring up from inside the boot, was John Wark. His eyes bulging, screaming blue murder behind the silver tape across his mouth.

ON THE STREET outside Christie's house, the senior investigating officer waved Winston over as soon as he had wrapped up his call to Grant.

'Anything from Grant?' he asked.

Winston shook his head convincingly. 'No, nothing.'

'Mr Winston, Duncan Grant murdered Ms Christie in cold blood. My guys are already saying this is an open and shut case against Duncan Grant. You'll let me know the second he's in contact. Right?'

Winston shot him a withering look of superiority. 'We're

MI6, inspector. We know how to find people. The second I know, you'll know.'

As the inspector walked off, he muttered out of earshot, 'Prick...'

Winston called Randall, who was still locked-down in his office. 'Did you get that?'

Typing away frantically on his computer, Randall confirmed, 'I traced the call to Lismore Street.'

'Lismore Street?' The name rang a bell.

Randall combed through satellite images of the area. 'Sir, I think he's in a lock-up under the arches.'

Winston ran towards his car while he spoke. 'Ping me the address. And Randall. Not a word to anyone.'

'It's already wiped from the network.'

'Good lad,' Winston said.

Once he was in the car, Winston checked that no one was looking. Then he took out a fifth of whisky he had just bought from a corner store on the way there.

Once the sting of the alcohol hit him, he sighed in relief.

'Come on, Leo,' he told himself. 'Keep it together.'

About to take another drink, he changed his mind. He screwed the cap back on and slid the bottle inside his coat pocket.

CHAPTER FORTY-EIGHT

Grant tossed a bucket of freezing water over Wark, who was tied to a wooden chair in the middle of the room.

Wark yelled behind the tape on his mouth. He was screaming his vocal cords raw.

Grant tapped him on the shoulder. 'Hey, hey, hey...you're wasting your time. Even if there was someone outside, they still couldn't hear you.'

Wark kept yelling, but with less intensity.

'What's the matter?' asked Grant. 'Don't like the bucket? That's what you get us to do on jobs. That and a whole lot worse.'

Faraday leaned back casually against the counter.

Wark looked to him for help.

'Don't look at me,' said Faraday. 'He's asking the questions.'

Grant crouched down in front of Wark, and snapped his fingers. 'Hey, listen to me...You're tied to this chair. No one knows you're here. No one's coming for you. All right? No one. It's going to be okay as long as you talk. Can you do that for me?'

Wark blinked hard, once, then nodded.

Grant continued, 'I'm going to take this tape off your mouth, and if you make noise…well, believe me when I say you'll regret it.' Grant ripped the tape off, prompting a yelp of pain from Wark.

'Please, please,' he begged. 'My wife. I have a wife and child.'

Faraday pointed out, 'So did Kadir Rashid.'

Grant shook his head in disgust. 'You think we just want to kill you? No, no. What we want to do is so much worse than that.'

Faraday went on, 'You told me he was a bomb maker.'

Wark shut his eyes. 'He was a national security risk.'

Grant said, 'He was a threat to your investment. You and the Crown Prince.'

'I'm not saying we didn't benefit, but it was geopolitical. It was complicated.'

'No it wasn't,' Grant fired back. 'It was calculated. You used the Albion programme to get rid of anyone who stood in the way of you turning a profit. Then when it all turned sour with Henry Marlow, you tried to bury it.'

Wark began to sob. 'I didn't mean…It wasn't my intention to–'

'Spare me the crocodile tears,' said Faraday.

As anguished as Wark was, he couldn't help his natural combative character shine through. 'You're a bloody fool, Faraday. I was going to make your life perfect. Whole again.'

'Then what was Sutherland about?'

'Sutherland was a mistake.'

'I'll say. You wanted rid of me and Grant. The two people who could name you as ordering the assassination of Rashid. Now that Downing Street is beckoning, you were clearing the table. Getting rid of the last remnants of evidence of AC one eighty, then killing everyone else who knew anything. Even Olivia Christie.'

'What about the others?' asked Grant.

'What others?' Wark replied.

'The other Albions. What did they ever do?'

'Their job,' he emphasised, trying to make them understand. 'That was the problem. They all knew too much. The days of secret programmes are over, Duncan. It was time to wrap Albion up for good. That meant leaving no trace.'

'You just ordered someone to kill them?'

'That's what we do,' Wark said. 'When something turns rotten, you don't leave little pieces of it around to fester. Eventually someone will smell it.'

'You weren't just mopping up the Rashid hit. It was the whole programme.'

'You don't get to be a part of something like Albion, having it come out when you're the Prime Minister and live to tell the tale. I've sacrificed too much to get this close. I wasn't going to let them stand in the way.'

Wark's head dropped. He was openly weeping now.

Grant lifted Wark's chin. 'Not nice on this side of the equation, is it? Much nicer in the palaces and townhouses and private members' club lounges. A bit more comfortable there.' Grant glanced down. 'You know you've pissed yourself? Did you know that?'

Wark's face was glazed with tears. 'If you want an apology, you won't get one. I'm not sorry. Not for any of it.'

Faraday cleared his throat, then brought over the retina scan box he'd taken from Christie's safe earlier that day. He held the box in front of Wark's face.

'There's no apology you could give me right now that I

would believe,' Grant told him. 'We've got everything we need in this box right here.' He grabbed Wark around the throat, then held open one of his eyes.

Faraday scanned Wark's eye with the box, which beeped assertively, then a small green LED lit up on the side. 'We're in,' he said, then took the box over to Marlow's laptop.

Grant came over to have a look. He nodded approvingly, then his thoughts turned to all the people who had died to keep the file a secret.

'What are you doing?' asked Wark, terrified to hear the answer.

'AC one eighty is going out to every major news outlet in the country. We'll start with that.'

Wark knew it was the end of the road. Still, he couldn't help but sound a note of defiance. 'You'll never get away with it. There's nowhere you can go that he won't find you.'

'Who?' asked Grant.

'Abdul. Who else?'

'You've got it all backwards, Wark,' he replied. 'There's nowhere that Abdul can go that I won't find him. I'm coming for him next.'

Faraday started assembling an email from a shell account, but he froze mid-typing.

There was a hard rap on the shutter.

Wark yelled out for help, rocking and swaying in his chair so hard that he tipped it over on its side. With no hands free to break his fall, his face smacked onto the bare concrete floor, smashing some teeth and leaving him spitting blood.

Grant hurried over and reapplied the silver tape across his mouth, but left him on his side. The noise hadn't prompted anything further from the shutter.

Faraday pulled out a gun, as did Grant.

They communicated silently, getting into position to tackle whoever was outside.

'Grant, it's me,' said the voice.

Grant squinted. 'It's Winston,' he told Faraday, then thought, *Is Winston slurring?*

Grant opened the shutter and pulled Winston inside quickly.

Winston froze when her saw a bloodied and bound John Wark tied to the upturned chair. 'Jesus...what the hell have you two done?' He turned to Faraday. 'And what's he doing here? I thought he was on Wark's side.'

'He's not,' said Grant.

'How do you know?'

'I just do. His story checks out.'

Winston paused. Staring at Wark, his eyes turned dark. Then he ran over and launched a series of volleys into Wark's stomach.

Powerless to stop him, Wark screeched in pain but no sound came out. Not even a muffled yelp. He was totally winded.

Grant and Faraday both rushed over to stop him.

'Hey, what the hell are you doing?' Grant yelled. He had his arms around Winston from the back, and pulled him away.

'Christie's dead because of him.'

'And the rest,' said Faraday.

Winston's eyes were wild, his blood clearly still up.

Grant gently slapped him on the cheek. 'Hey, cool off. We're here for answers.'

Winston backed off, running a hand over the top of his head.

Being in proximity to Winston was enough for Grant to know what was up. As a teetotaller, it was even more obvious.

'Leo, have you been drinking?' asked Grant.

'No,' he said, unconvinced.

'You're slurring your words. And you smell of cheap whisky.'

Winston huffed. 'I had a drink, all right? You'd have a drink too if you'd been stabbed in the stomach like me.'

Grant turned his head slightly in confusion. 'What do you mean? Christie?'

Winston waved haphazardly. He was drunker than he had seemed at first. Years of hiding it from the agency had fine-tuned his abilities. 'What about AC one eighty? Do we have it?'

Faraday said, 'Yeah, we have—'

Grant cut in, 'Robert!'

'What is it?' asked Winston.

Grant stood still for a moment, then he drew his weapon quickly and pointed it at Winston.

Faraday nearly jumped out of his skin. 'Duncan, what are you doing? Have you lost your mind?'

Grant stared hard at Winston. 'Leo...I'm going to ask you a very simple question. And I want you to think long and hard about the answer before you speak. Do you understand me?'

Winston raised his hands, and chuckled in disbelief. 'Duncan, what is this? It's me!' Seeing Grant unbending, Winston looked in desperation to Faraday. 'Tell him, Robert! Tell him!'

Worried that something had snapped in Grant, Faraday said, 'I don't know what's happening either. But Grant, look at me. Talk to me.'

Grant said to Faraday by the laptop, 'Look up Leo's personnel file. It's there on the network. The debriefing report when he returned from China.'

'China?' said Winston, baffled. 'What is all this?'

'You'll see,' said Grant.

Faraday scrolled through the report, a densely packed wall of text. He shook his head. 'I need a little more, Duncan. What am I looking for here?'

'Look up "stomach",' said Grant.

Winston gulped hard.

Grant didn't take his eyes off him. Finger on the trigger.

Faraday found the search word. 'The Chinese stabbed his stomach. So what?'

Still staring at Winston, Grant said, 'I thought it strange that Christie was killed by a stomach wound. If death was the only goal, there are dozens of quicker ways. Was it really about inflicting as much pain as possible? That's when I remembered, in your debriefing.' He turned to Faraday, 'Scroll down. There's a picture.'

Faraday found it. It was a picture of Leo's stomach, a thick pink scar where the Chinese had stabbed him.

Grant explained, 'The same place Christie was stabbed.'

'This is crazy,' Winston pleaded. 'As if we're the only two people to ever be stabbed in the stomach.'

'It's not a hit, though. Is it? It's vengeful, killing someone like that.'

'What are you saying, Duncan?'

'You two had made a pact in China. That if either one of you was captured, you'd shoot the other to spare them the MSS' torture methods. Knowing it could drag on for months, it might have seemed ghoulish to an outsider, but when you've seen what the MSS do to enemy agents, you would beg someone to shoot you. To spare you that punishment. That agony. For months at a time.'

Winston's posture softened. He turned his back, shaking his head. 'I can't believe I'm listening to this...'

Faraday was still all ears. Rapt with where Grant was going with it all.

Grant continued, 'When you were captured, she had a chance to shoot you. But she couldn't do it. She wasn't cut out for it. Couldn't shoot her friend, regardless of your pleas. That's what you told me. You begged her to shoot you.'

'I understood!' claimed Winston. 'I forgave her.'

'I don't believe you,' Grant replied. 'It was the reason you drank. I don't think you ever forgave her. It's not the whole reason why you turned, Leo, but it's a good part of it. What I can't figure out is why you turned on me too.'

Having been locked into shock and disbelief since Grant had pulled his gun, Winston attempted to shift into the denial stage. 'Duncan, I would never betray you. *Ever.*'

Grant heard the words, but they meant nothing to him. 'You told me once that you don't ever open your mouth unless you know what the shot is. You can park all the fancy surveillance techniques, the guns, the gadgets. But fundamentally, the spy game often comes down to two people sitting in a room talking. Or maybe a hospital room.' Grant leaned forward accusingly, speaking precisely, emphasising each part of the rule. 'You never open your mouth, unless you *know* what the shot is.'

Having run through the gamut of emotions, something inside Winston finally snapped. He'd run through the denial phase, jumped straight over anger and bargaining, and had now landed squarely on acceptance. 'You've obviously made up your mind.'

Grant said, 'In case you're wondering, it was the Ridley thing.'

'What Ridley thing?' asked Faraday.

Grant explained, 'When I visited Leo in hospital the other

night and I told him I would be working with Ridley, he claimed that he didn't know him, and had never met him. Yet, if you open up Ridley's acquisition file, it's filled out by none other than Leo Winston.'

Faraday found it on he network and checked. 'He's right,' he told Winston, showing him the screen. 'There's a photo and everything.'

Winston shrugged impotently. 'Do you have any idea how many operatives I've recruited in my time? They all look like Ridley, for crying out loud!'

Grant continued, 'Which I might have overlooked in isolation. But during our journey north to Sutherland, Ridley claimed to me that he had never met you either. One of you forgetting or being mistaken is possible. But both of you? The only explanation is that you were both lying. And why would both of you be lying?'

Winston shook his head like he was having to tolerate the words of a mad person.

Grant went on, 'Both of you were trying to distance yourselves from each other. Because you were both part of the same conspiracy: to send me on a suicide mission to extract Faraday, killing him in the process too.'

Winston pleaded to Faraday, 'You can't possibly believe all this? Something has snapped in him since Marlow. Since Gretchen was killed.' He turned to Grant, 'I get it. I know what grief can do to you.'

Faraday didn't look convinced though.

Grant said, 'There's a simple way to prove it. Let's ask Wark.'

Faraday said, 'I don't know, Duncan. You can't exactly trust what he has to say. He'd say anything you want to hear right now.'

'Exactly,' Winston said.

No to be outdone, Grant said, 'Well, if you still want proof, what will Randall find if I ask him to check the flight logs at RAF Buchan? Will he find a chartered flight taken by you Leo, to search my cottage in my absence? You knew where I kept my knife, but you didn't know that I'd taken it with me. When I came back, I put my knife in its usual place. Yet somehow, Christie knew where it was. Only you could have told her. If she'd known that the very same knife would end up being used to kill her, she might not have been as forthcoming with her help. But you and Christie had been told by Wark to find something to set me up. Christie thought she was going to be fired. With her out the picture, Wark could elevate you to Director, and he would have a perfect puppet in place running the agency. Because Christie running the show with him in Downing Street was going to be a never-ending headache. And he knew it. Wark roped her in too, but she tried to kick out. By then it was too late. Wark wasn't going to leave her walking around and available to be interrogated at a foreign select committee. No, if all the Albions had to go, then so did she. She knew that Wark had you bought and paid for. What did he threaten you with? Expulsion? Expose your drinking to standards and practices? He blackmailed you. Dangled the job that was the only thing keeping your life together in front of you–'

Winston interjected, 'Do I actually get to speak during this diatribe?'

Grant stared hard at him. 'You never open your mouth unless you know what the shot is.' A long pause, while Grant trembled with rage inside. 'You broke my heart, Leo...'

Winston had been keeping it together for so long. But Grant was about to break him.

He said, 'You were like a father to me. I wish I could believe you didn't know Wark had sent Ridley on that op to kill me...'

Winston shook his head sombrely. 'I swear I didn't, Duncan...I tried to warn you to stay away. Wark threatened to expose my drinking. They'd already suspended me when you went AWOL. I didn't have a choice...'

'There's always a choice,' Grant replied.

Winston nodded. 'That's true.'

While Grant's defences were down, Winston snatched for something at his back waistband, pulling out a Walther PDP, ideal for concealed carry.

But Grant didn't flinch.

Winston was pointing the gun under his own chin. 'If you'd rather shoot me first Duncan, I won't resist. God knows I deserve it. I've got nothing left to live for anyway.'

'I know that's what Wark is counting on. For me to kill you in revenge and clear the slate for him. I won't do it.'

Winston pursed his lips. 'That's what I feared...'

He pressed the gun harder against his chin, but before he could pull the trigger Grant shot a single round into his chest. Winston tried to pull the trigger anyway, but the impact from Grant's shot had launched his head backwards just in time, sending the bullet into the roof.

Winston lay sprawled on the floor, twitching and gasping for breath.

Grant ran to him. 'Call it in,' he yelled to Faraday.

Faraday paused. 'Call it in? What about us? Everyone still thinks you killed Christie.'

'Maybe that's the way it has to be,' Grant answered. He leaned down to Winston's ear. 'Help's on the way, Leo.'

Winston groaned, trying to say something.

Grant hoped that it was 'sorry'. He certainly looked like he was saying it with his eyes.

Grant concluded by saying, 'But this is where I say goodbye.'

Faraday had gathered up Marlow's laptop, along with some weapons and clean burner phones. 'Grant,' he snapped. 'Come *on*, we have to go.'

Grant stood up. 'You called it in?'

'They'll be here in two minutes.'

Grant took one look back at Wark who was quietly sobbing, knowing his career would be over by the time Grant and Faraday's AC-180 leak had hit the news outlets.

Then Grant looked at Winston. For a moment he considered staying behind. But that would mean sacrificing himself before he had completed his mission. There was still one piece left.

EPILOGUE
SIX WEEKS LATER

Leo stood at a fold-up table set up at the back of the church hall, where metal coffee jugs and plastic cups had been laid out. There was an apparent neutrality to AA when it came to belief in any divine spirit. The wording in the famous Twelve Steps had left an ingenious loophole to get non-believers off the hook.

That, "we made a decision to turn our will and our lives over to the care of God as we understood him."

Leo couldn't help but admire that last "as we understood him". It seemed pretty clear – from his occasional forays into the world of AA – that the serious guys that ran meetings and spread the word were fully invested in the idea of God. They were true believers.

Leo was not a true believer. He flinched at every mention of something religious during an AA meeting. As far as he was concerned, it was easy to believe in God when you had overcome your addictions, and were so well put together that you were able to admit in front of strangers all the terrible things you had done, and to offer help to others.

It was much harder to believe in God when you were practically crawling to the off-licence five minutes before opening time so you could get in and buy your booze within the earliest minute legally possible – because you had woken up shaking so badly that you literally thought you were going to die. God doesn't seem quite so easily accessible in moments like that.

Moments of the kind that Leo had survived in recent weeks.

He poured some coffee, and wondered if it would be bad form to tip in some of the whisky in his pocket. Surely, if there was one place where that would be acceptable it was in an AA meeting. Still, he managed to resist.

The meeting itself was the usual Leo had sat through recently. One old timer was finishing off his 'share'.

The man – a white sticker on his chest identified him as Harry – said, '...and now all I feel is intense gratitude that the obsession has finally left me, and I was able to find you guys, and this meeting, and God.'

Everyone clapped, but Leo lagged behind the others – and he clapped much less enthusiastically.

He didn't understand people like Harry. It actually made him angry. People who were that together. It seemed to Leo that people like Harry should have had their own meeting. Alcoholics Anonymous And People Who Don't Really Have Problems Anymore.

The group leader asked, 'Anyone else like to share this week?'

Leo, slumped in his chair, raised his hand. 'Yeah, I'll go.'

The others watched him with a mix of pity and sadness. They could hear the booze at work in his voice. And the smell, of course, gave him away.

Leo began, 'It's nice that some of you guys don't drink

anymore, and you've got over it. That must be nice. But honestly?' He said it gently, without a trace of malice. 'Fuck you. Fuck the lot of you. You're grateful? What are you grateful for? Fucking your life up? Congratulations.' The gentility in his voice now vanished. Morphing into frustration, and then anger. 'The obsession left you? You don't want to drink? Guess what, I'm sitting here, I want a drink. You're not an alcoholic, I am. Because I want a goddamn *drink*.' He stabbed a finger downwards in the air. 'I'm drunk *now*!'

No one knew where to look. But it would be bad form to interject. So everyone sat there and waited for Leo to work it out.

'Sorry,' Leo murmured. 'It's just...you can win a thousand days, and all it takes is that one day where you cave. Where you have that drink...'

Cue a lot of nodding heads around the room.

'I've been doing this for a while now, and it's become clear to me that the only way to cure yourself of this shit is to suffer enough. Eventually, your life turns to enough types of shit, that you decide you can't do it anymore. That if you want to salvage what's left of your life, you have to decide. No one tells you. You have to decide...' he hesitated to say it, but he really did believe it. 'I think I'm finally there. And it took me ruining the closest thing I ever had to a son. And in the process, I also took away a father figure to someone who needed it. Now I'll probably never see that person again. I thought about killing myself. I've tried it before, but this time I would do it properly. But then I thought, actually, the more honourable thing do is to live with the pain that I've caused myself. And maybe, if I'm lucky, I'll get a chance to make amends.' Leo turned to Harry. 'And Harry...you know what. That would make me grateful.'

Harry nodded to him in appreciation.

It felt strange walking home in the middle of the afternoon on a weekday. His suspension from MI6 still ongoing, but he already felt unemployed. The world was moving on without him. The story of what had become known as 'The Rashid Files' was still taking up acres of column inches in national newspapers even weeks after John Wark's resignation from Cabinet and soon after as an MP – owing to a pending police investigation into the events detailed in MI6 Anticorruption File 180.

Winston glanced towards the off-licence he often stopped in on, but kept walking today.

A young boy who should have been in school collided with him, then shot him a nasty look.

Moments later, Winston was still looking back at the boy when he heard a phone ring. He looked down his front in confusion, then to the sides. The phone was on him somewhere. Which should have been impossible, because he hadn't taken a phone out with him.

He patted down his pockets, then felt the unexpected bulge of a phone in his front jacket pocket. A grudging smile cross his face as he remembered the young boy. He answered it.

'Who's this?' he asked tentatively.

'It's me.'

Winston immediately halted. He would have known the voice anywhere. 'Duncan...I...I–'

'It's all right, Leo. You don't have to say anything.'

'I want to.'

'Where are you?'

'Home. But not for long. I wanted to let you know. I'm

putting together a team. There's a little project I've been working on. I need you.'

'What do you need me for?' Winston asked.

'I need you back in MI6. You know what that means?'

'That I need to get cleaned up.'

'If you want to help. I figured you might want a piece of it. Faraday's in. I'm about to call Randall.'

Winston shook his head gently. 'You're really going after him, aren't you?'

'It's time, Leo. It was always going to end this way. I've already started.'

'I don't know, Duncan. There's a new boss at MI6 these days. I've still got a chance of coming back in if I'm lucky. And I stay dry.'

'If you're not with me, then I need you to get a message to MI6.'

'Saying what?'

'Don't get in my way.'

Winston looked around. 'Duncan, what have you got yourself into?'

'I want you to tell them not to get in my way. I'm going to burn it all down, Leo.'

Winston shut his eyes and pinched his temples. 'You sound just like him. Do you know that? You sound like Marlow.'

'It's very simple this time, Leo,' Grant explained. 'Tell MI6 you're either with me or against me.'

He hung up.

When Winston got home, there was a black Rolls Royce waiting outside his house. A man in a mackintosh coat got out and put up an umbrella against the heavy rain that was falling.

Winston slowed his walk as he approached, wondering what the man wanted with him. 'This is, uh...a surprise, sir.'

He said, 'We need to talk, Winston. There's a situation in Saudi Arabia. I need you back.'

Winston exhaled, unsure how he felt about such a request. 'Honestly, sir, I don't know if I'm ready to come back yet.'

'We've received intel from Fifteen Flags. They've received evidence of a credible threat against Crown Prince Muhammad bin Abdul.' The man paused gravely. 'Winston, the evidence suggests it's one of our own going after him. Can you help?'

Winston bit his lower lip, thinking about the talk at the AA meeting about making amends. 'Yes, sir.' He began to smile. 'I think I can help.'

EPILOGUE

Grant took one last wander through the cottage he had called home as long as he could remember. The place had long since been stripped of anything resembling family mementoes. It could have been a stranger that had lived there since Grant's mum and dad had died.

In a way, it had been a stranger. Their deaths had changed Grant irrevocably. Once he had felt able to move on from his grief – particularly after his mother's death, which happened much earlier in Grant's life – he almost felt sorry for the other kids in school who wouldn't lose anyone close to them until well into adulthood. Such loss would cripple them. But for Grant, it prepared him for what the world could throw at you.

It also taught him the valuable lesson that change is not only good. It's necessary.

As was so often the case in life, the most rewarding change can happen when life forces you to change against your will.

It happened when Grant's mother had died. And the same had happened throughout the whole Henry Marlow episode, and again when Grant lost Gretchen Winter out in that Saudi oilfield.

And now it was happening again, except this time, he was forcing the change himself. He knew it was time.

What he needed to do now, demanded that he disappear into the darkest void. For him to succeed, there could be no more Duncan Grant.

It wasn't about trying to fake his own death. He just needed to make a clean break from the past. And there was only one clear way he could think of doing that.

He took the can of petrol and doused the living room, then the kitchen, then left a trail of fuel down the short hallway and out the door to the garden.

He stood where the line of fuel stopped on the grass and he took out a lighter. He knew that once it was done there would be no going back. Which was the way he wanted it. It would be saying goodbye to the last vestiges of who he was and had been.

He flicked the lighter on, then dropped it onto the fuel. The flames licked up in the breeze, running quickly back into the cottage, where the flames burst into life in the living room.

In a few moments, the fire had engulfed the whole cottage. Swallowing it. Consuming it.

Grant turned his back on it without a word, then got into his car. As he drove along the winding path leading to the main road, he could see the fire spreading to the roof, black smoke billowing up, and blown sideways by a stiff westerly wind off the coast.

In the minute or so it took to reach the road, Grant didn't so much as sneak a look in the rear-view mirror.

On the passenger seat next to him was the photo of Gretchen Winter that had once adorned his living room wall.

As the cottage burned down behind him, Grant glanced at the photo and said, 'It's time to even the score.'

And MI6 were either going to be with him, or against him.

Printed in Great Britain
by Amazon